DICK WONDERCOCK

AND THE

DEFECTIVE DETECTIVE

I hope you been through this story!

Keith Fire

A Story by Keith Fire

1

"Welcome. What can I get you?" asked Laura. She was the manager and head bartender at Harry's Hideaway, a hotel bar in the downtown area. The customer who had just walked in was a woman in her late thirties. She had a brown mullet and wore a faded flannel shirt with old blue jeans.

"That was a hell of a drive. I guess I'll take a beer," the woman said.

"Which beer do you want?"

"Uh, what do you have?"

"Pretty much everything. It's a good selection."

"All right. I'll take a Miller Lite draft, then," she said, trying to read the taps from six stools away. She had her left eye closed. Laura thought she looked like a lumberjack pirate. "Oh, and I need you to throw a little Bloody Mary mix in there."

"You want the mix in the beer?"

"Yeah. Never had that. Good shit."

"Sure," Laura said and went to the taps. She grabbed a pint glass from the back bar in a fluid motion on her way by. She tilted the tapper forward and reached underneath the bar to get the Zing Zang from the refrigerator. She splashed a little in, watching it swirl down as the glass filled. She thought it looked awful.

"Hey," said a man with a croaky voice. Laura looked up, but he was focused on another patron who was wearing a Patrick Mahomes jersey. "Where'd you get that Chiefs tattoo?"

"In Kansas City. Arrowhead Tattoos. Why?"

"Just wondering. I knew a guy that had a Queen of Hearts. Matching colors, you know. Thought maybe you two knew each other."

"Because we both have red tattoos?"

"Yeah, hey, I'm Tommy Bowlin. What's your name?"

"I'm Peter Bayless," the man said, looking like he had fallen into a ripe dumpster.

"Peter Bayless? Sounds familiar. Yeah. Just like that guy from Game of Thrones? Have you seen that?"

"I think that's Baelish, but yeah, it's similar, I guess."

"You've seen it?"

"Sure have. Hated the last season though."

"Yeah, I'll agree with that. Needed a little more of that white headed dragon lady showing off her boobs."

"Daenerys? She didn't really do that."

"Right. That's why there should have been more of it. At least we have the dragon house show to look forward to."

"House of the Dragon? Yeah. I watched most of the first season. It's terrible."

"But are there more boobs?" Tommy asked, his eyes bulging with anticipation.

"I don't know," Peter said, slowly turning away." Can I get another scotch?"

"Be right there!" Laura called from the other end of the bar. "Dewars, right?"

"Yep."

"Hey, bartender," called a man that was part of a group at a high-top table. "Where's our waitress? We're about to dry up and blow away over here."

"Jen? I don't know. Let me check after I make this drink."

"Fine, but we need beer soon! Maybe a discount on the next round."

Laura ignored that, poured the scotch, and set it in front of Peter with a fresh napkin.

"Thanks," he said.

"You got some laundry going back there?" Tommy asked.

"What?"

"Sounds like a pair of shoes in a dryer. Bang, bang, banging' away."

4

"Jen!" Laura said, walking around the corner to a short hallway where the storeroom, employee bathroom, and her office were located. "Jen! Where the hell are you?"

The banging was louder, and she knew what was happening. The door to the storeroom was locked. She pounded on it.

"God damn it, Jen!" Laura said, reaching for the elastic band that held her keys.

"Hold on!" called a man's voice.

"You're on the clock!"

"No," he said, grunting. "She's on the table."

"Gotta be fucking kidding me right now. You have customers, Jen!"

"Almost done… almost…. Aaahhhh," he said, and the banging stopped.

Laura heard some shuffling inside and the door opened. Jen offered a sheepish grin and slipped off toward the bathroom, tugging her skirt back into place. That left Laura staring at a man whose pants were still bulging but fastened. He was buttoning his long-sleeve shirt. He looked up at her as his hands went up to smooth down his dark brown hair. He had perfect teeth with a smile that reminded her of Matthew McConaughey. He had no facial hair and it looked like he must have shaved late in the day because he didn't have the slightest shadow. She couldn't decide if the dimple in his left cheek or his sparkling blue eyes were cuter.

"What the fuck?" she asked.

"I think you know the answer to that," he said, looking at his reflection in an old bar mirror.

"Who are you?"

"I'm Dick. Dick Wondercock."

"You just go around fucking waitresses during their shift with some fake ass name?"

"It's my real name," he said. He took his suit coat from the corner of a metal rack and pulled a wallet from its pocket. He

5

flipped it open to reveal his credentials, which showed the name Dick Wondercock. "One hundred percent."

"All right, Dick. Stay the hell out of my waitress's pants while she's working, ok?"

"I couldn't wait."

"You certainly could have. Now she's got pissed off customers."

"I'll buy them a round and they'll be fine. Probably those assholes at the high top."

"Good guess," Laura said, turning away. "Hey, do me a favor."

"What's that?" Dick asked, putting his jacket back on.

"If you're going to pull out, at least clean that cum off the floor. Mop's over there."

"Yes, ma'am."

"Make sure you rinse it out, too. I don't want to find a crusty mop when we get ready to clean the place tonight."

When Dick walked back out into the bar area, he looked perfect. His suit didn't have a single wrinkle and his hair was exactly right. Jen was at the high top, apologizing to the men. Her face was still flushed.

"Gentlemen," Dick said, joining her. "My apologies for making you wait a few minutes for a beer. This round is on me. Add that to my tab, please."

Jen looked up at him, smiled, and rushed off to put in the order. The men were staring at him. He patted one of them on the shoulder.

"You think buying us a round offsets the poor service? Gonna take more than that to make me happy."

"Friend, I don't claim to know what could possibly make you happy and her service has been just fine until that little blip, right? Don't worry though, I'm sure you're not going to tip her, so I handled that already."

"I could kick your ass right now," said the man opposite him. He was chubby, bald, and his cheeks were rosy.

"I doubt that," Dick said, offering a sympathetic smile. "No need for violence though. The game is on, and you all surely have something good to talk about that doesn't involve me or your waitress."

"What a dick," another one of them said.

"Yes, I am. Now, you all be nice to her. Got it?" Dick asked. He wore a smile, but the intensity of the situation shone clearly in his eyes.

"Leave us alone."

"That'll do," Dick said and went to a booth along the front wall.

He wanted to be able to see anyone coming in. Jen started his way, but Laura grabbed her by the arm and shook her head. Jen went off toward one of her other tables.

"You're staying, then?" Laura asked when she got to his table.

"If you don't mind."

"Just here for the scenery or are you buying something else?"

"I'll take a double Jameson on the rocks. Rest assured that I will not interfere with Jen's shift any more than I already have."

"I told her to steer clear. Her shift is over in forty minutes," Laura said, finding it hard to stay upset with him.

"When's your shift over?"

"Can't dip your pen in two inkwells at the same bar. I'm sure you know that rule."

"Well, yes. Unless they aren't at the same bar at the same time, or they are both ok with it."

"I'll be right back with your drink."

"Thank you."

Dick scanned the room. The crowd was still light, but he assumed it would pick up before long. He checked his watch. If his intel was good, his target would arrive soon. Laura came back with the drink.

"There you go. Double Jameson on the rocks. Anything else I can get you?"

"I mean…"

"Food, drinks, appetizers, or dessert. Nothing else is on the menu."

"Got it. I'm good for now."

"Enjoy," she said and went back to the bar.

The table of assholes seemed to have settled back into their conversation. He'd be watching how they treated Jen at the next round. There was only one guy at the bar at that point. He was talking at Laura in his croaky voice while also looking around. He locked eyes with Dick for a moment, but then looked away a split second later. Two couples sat in booths, and another held a group of women that looked like they were out for ladies' night. He considered stopping there before he left. He'd find at least one who didn't need to get right home.

"Hey, Mr. Cooper," Jen said, greeting a new customer at the door.

"Hey, kiddo. Is my booth open?"

"Sure is. I put the reserved sign on it about an hour ago. Wasn't sure if you'd be in, but I thought you would."

"You can count on me," he said.

He wore a gray wool fedora, which he took off when Jen gestured toward the table in question. With the hat off, his full head of white hair came into view. The matching gray overcoat hung open, showing a suit that looked like it needed a good cleaning. The white stubble on his face appeared to be a few days old.

"Old fashioned?" she asked.

"Me or the drink?" Cooper asked with a melancholy smile.

"Oh, Mr. Cooper, you're silly. I'll have your drink up in just a minute."

8

"Sounds good," he said and walked to the back corner.

The booth was round and could easily seat seven. Cooper took off his coat and hung it on a silver hook at the end of the booth. He slid around to the spot in the back middle. He placed his hat on the seat next to him. Jen leaned across the table to place a napkin and his drink in front of him. Dick had a long look.

"Anything else, right now?"

"Let me get a couple of these in me. Then, I'll probably need a firehouse cheeseburger."

"With sweet potato fries and extra jalapenos?"

"That'll be perfect. I'll let you know when I'm ready."

"Good enough," she said and walked away. She saw Dick watching her and gave him a wink.

Cooper sipped at his drink, reading the flip menu on the table that showed the drink specials. He never ordered anything else, but it was something to do. His phone rang, sounding like an old-time phone with an actual bell in it. He pulled it from his pants pocket, flipped it open, and held it out in an attempt to read the caller ID.

"To hell with that," he said and slapped it down on the table.

"Is this seat taken?" Dick asked, standing in front of the booth with his drink in hand.

"No, but I'm not really looking for conversation tonight. Not really looking for it any night."

"I understand," Dick said. "This isn't a social call though."

"Just what I fucking need. Are you a fan? A reporter? A lawyer?"

"You are Carland Cooper, right?"

"What are you? A process server? You look too well dressed for that."

"No, sir, I'm not. My name is Dick Wondercock. I'm a private investigator."

"Dick Wondercock? That has to be the funniest thing I've heard in a while."

"I've got credentials, if you want them."

"Hell, no. I just want to enjoy my drink. Leave me be, ok?"

"Like I said, this isn't a social call. I'm on the clock right now. Your daughter, Carla, hired me."

"Carla?" he asked. He started swirling his drink a bit and then looked up. "What'd she hire you to do?"

"Do you mind if I sit?"

"Might as well. You obviously aren't leaving."

"That's right, sir."

"Look, can you drop the sir shit? I get that all day at work. I know I'm old and probably need to retire, but I can't bring myself to it. My wife died ten years ago. My only kid is busy in another state. Not much left to do if I hang it up."

"Makes sense. I don't think I'd quit, either."

"Private detective, huh?"

"Yep. Been doing it since I got out of the service."

"Oh, yeah? What branch?"

"Doesn't matter. That was a long time ago."

"Can't be more than ten years judging by your looks."

"Fourteen. I was in for five. You can do the math from there."

"Right. So, what does Carla want you to do?"

"Investigate."

"A smartass, too. I'm really winning today."

"She said you've been struggling at work. Bit of a cold streak, I guess. She said you called her after you'd been here one night last week and told her you had lost your touch."

"I remember. I wasn't as drunk as she thought."

Dick pulled out his phone and tapped the screen. He scrolled down a page before nodding.

"You said you were a 'defective detective'."

"Maybe I was drunker than I thought."

10

"Anyway. She's concerned that your downslide in luck at work might be affecting your overall disposition."

"Downslide in luck? Buddy, it ain't no downslide. I haven't solved anything in close to a year!" Cooper said before downing the rest of his drink. Jen walked over.

"Ready for another?"

"If I leave, are you coming with me?" Cooper asked Dick.

"I'm afraid so."

"I'll have another, then."

"Don't you run off my best tipper," she said.

"I thought I was your best tipper."

"Shut up," she said playfully. "Looks like you need another one, too."

"Yeah, I'll have one more. Put his on my bill."

"That's not necessary."

"I can write it off."

"Fine."

"Ok, so tell me about this cold streak."

"Not much to it. I've always had a really high close rate. Last year, things slowed down and then dried up. Other guys are still clipping along, but my stuff is dead."

"What have you been investigating?"

"I've been on white collar stuff for a while. I'd say twenty years."

"That's not sexy."

"Hey, I've seen enough bodies in alleys and people in hospitals after taking a beating to last a lifetime. Not going to say these cases are harmless, but a lot less blood."

"I guess that's true. So, why do you come here?" Dick asked as Jen returned with drinks. She slid them into place and walked away. "This isn't your typical cop bar."

"That's exactly why I come here."

"And Jen?"

"She's a good kid. She's about the same age as my oldest grandson."

"You should set her up with him."

"I might not be doing well at work, but I can see the way she looks at you. I'd rather not put my grandson in that. Besides, he's halfway across the country."

"I'm harmless."

"I doubt that."

"Here's what I want to do. I'd like to set up a time for us to talk when you're ready. Maybe tomorrow afternoon? I kind of sprang it on you tonight."

Cooper's phone rang again. He didn't bother trying to read it, instead electing to flip it open.

"What?"

Dick could hear a man's voice, but it was nothing more than a hum of distant words. Cooper hung up as soon as the man stopped talking.

"Fucking children."

"Carla?"

"What?" Cooper said, looking at him. "Oh, no, she never acted like these guys. It's one of the newer officers that wrote the initial report on a case assigned to me. He insists on calling me Coop, as if we are buddies. He'd probably forget his name if his mommy didn't write it on the inside of his underwear."

"I like that."

"Tomorrow afternoon is fine. Let's say 3:30. Meet here?"

"No," Dick said. "Let's go to the Ironclad."

"Jesus. That place is a hole."

"It's near the station, though."

"You want me to take you to the station? That's not happening."

"Not tomorrow. We need to cover more info first."

"I can't march a P.I. into a police station and let him start looking around."

12

"Fine. That's not what I'm asking for," Dick said. "I want to go to the Ironclad because I want to see how other cops act around you. I know that it's a pretty regular hangout for the guys at your precinct."

"Yeah. I used to go there a lot. The last two months, I've only been coming here."

"We'll just go there once and see what happens."

"Nothing is going to happen. It's full of cops."

"I get it."

"Look, I don't know what your end goal is here, but I don't want you soaking my daughter for a bunch of money. I've just lost my touch. Nothing more."

"Mr. Cooper, I'm not soaking your daughter for anything. She gave me a twenty percent retainer, but that's all."

"If you're going to be doing this, I don't want you to be calling me Mr. Cooper. He's on a hill north of the city. I go by Carl."

"Got it, Carl. So, let's meet at the Ironclad at 3:30 tomorrow. I'll dress down a little."

"Probably a good idea. They'll be suspicious enough of a guy they don't know talking to me."

"I'm going to let you have your booth back. I appreciate your time," Dick said, standing up. "Oh, don't worry about your daughter too much. If I don't deliver a solution, she doesn't pay the balance."

"Must be hard to make a living like that."

"Nah, I'm that good," Dick said. His pearly whites gleamed in the low light. "Have a good night, Carl."

"I'll do my best, Dick."

He walked back to the bar, where Tommy Bowlin had engaged another solo drinker in a meaningless discussion. Dick tipped his glass back and swallowed the rest of his drink. He looked at it and put it on the bar. Laura started his way. He placed three crisp fifties on the bar in front of her.

"I'll get your change."

"Split it with Jen."

"Maybe I will and maybe I won't," she said with mischief in her eyes.

"You're the boss," he said. He put on his hat, straightened his jacket, and went to the front door. He took another glance at Jen, who was stuck at the high-top with the assholes. She smiled at him, and he tipped his hat.

2

City Storage stood across the road from the Ironclad. It had seven rows of buildings with storage units in them. At the back was a lot where people stored campers, equipment, and extra vehicles. In the third to last space along the right side, a blue quad cab truck was parked. It wasn't a paying customer. It was Dick Wondercock.

He was in the spot directly behind the driver's seat with his suit pants down to his knees. A woman with long blonde hair was stretched across the bench seat with her head slowly sliding up and down in his lap. She had started off making slurping and gagging sounds, but he assured her that was unnecessary.

"Just like that," he said, and laid his head back against the glass. "That's really good, Olivia."

She lifted her head slightly and said, "Thanks."

Otherwise, she didn't miss a beat. He gave a little twitch, and she took that as a sign to speed up. He grabbed her by the ass and thrust up. She held her place. That brought their tryst to a quick end.

"Holy shit," he said and sank back down.

She grabbed a tissue from the box on the floor and wiped her mouth.

"I definitely got the better end of that deal," he said.

"Hey, you got the address you wanted for one of my renters and I got to do that. I'm good with it."

"Got to? That's a first."

"You don't know us women as well as you might like to think."

"I'm confident in that," he said and pulled his pants back up. "How long is your lunch break?"

"Not long enough," she said. "You need to stop by again sometime."

"I think that can be arranged."

"Good. Now, take me back up front. I gotta brush my teeth before I get any customers."

"Always prepared."

"Having a toothbrush is not exactly being prepared for this, but that's ok."

"Better than ok," he said and opened his door. He stepped down onto the running board and closed the door. He got in the driver's seat. She got in the passenger seat next to him.

"So, what did Jack Nelson do?"

"What do you mean?"

"You needed his address or at least that's what you said."

"Well, I needed the address that he gave you."

"Why?"

"Not completely sure yet. That's what I'm getting paid to find out."

"Some extracurricular activities that his wife is tracking down?"

"I think it's something less exciting than what you are imagining."

"You seem to like extracurricular activities, too."

"This is purely curricular," he said, offering her a smile that made her blush. He started the truck and drove toward the entrance.

"Where are you off to next?" she asked. "Some other lovely lady?"

"Far from it. Going right across the street."

She scrunched her nose and said, "That's a cop bar. Doesn't seem like the kind of place Jack would go to."

"First, you have to forget that I asked about John Nelson, Jr. Second, I have more than one case at a time. One of the others is taking me over there."

"Can I join you when I'm done here?"

"That's not going to work."

"Please," she said with a pout.

16

"I'm meeting a client. I won't forget you. We'll get a drink somewhere a little nicer someday."

"I guess that'll have to be good enough," she said and opened the door.

"Have a good rest of your day," he said.

"Eh, I'll probably just watch videos on my phone."

She hopped out and closed the door. She offered a short wave before going inside. After unlocking the door, she turned to look at him and was happy to see him still watching her. He rolled the truck forward, checked for traffic, and crossed the road.

There were no marked squad cars in the lot, but he counted four dark blue Taurus sedans and two white ones. He found it amusing that these guys owned regular versions of the cars they drove for work. Then again, he had gotten hooked on trucks while he was in the military. He had almost no practical use for this one, but he liked it.

"Let's see," he said after he backed into a parking spot facing the building. It was a concrete block building with small windows. Each one was secured with black iron bars. He looked at his notes to see what kind of vehicle Carl drove. "A silver 2017 Lincoln Continental. Nice choice."

He looked around and didn't see one of those, but it was only a quarter after three. The Detective was probably a punctual man, if nothing else. He decided to go in and find a seat. He imagined a dark place with booths around the perimeter and an old bar along one long wall. Probably four taps and a simple shelf of liquors.

Dick locked his truck and went to the steel door that had been painted black. The word 'ENTRANCE' was stenciled in white on it. When he opened the door, he realized he wasn't too far off. The light seemed to flood the dark room. Six men at the bar all turned to look at him. Two guys playing pool did the same.

"Close the fucking door!"

17

Dick pulled it shut behind him and made his way to a high-top along the end of the room closest to the street. It was the pedestal style and had two beer coasters jammed under one side to keep it from rocking. The top was laminate that looked like wood, but the matching edge had been torn off long ago. He picked a chair that gave him a view of the door.

"Honey," the bartender said. "If you want something to drink then you have to come up here. I don't do no table service."

She was tall with black hair cut into a bob. She wore a plain white T-shirt with a denim vest over it. Dick didn't think she was bad looking in general, but he'd rather make a trip back to see Oliva than attempt anything with her.

"Right," he said and went to the end of the bar. He glanced at the six men, who were clearly cops. They all had matching haircuts and five had mustaches of basically the same style. The last one had a goatee. They each had a Natural Light. "Got any Natty Light?"

"No one likes a smartass," the guy with the goatee said.

"Shut the fuck up, Chris," the bartender said. "If I didn't like smartasses, I'd have to throw all of you out."

"Come on, Pam. We're just busting his balls. People don't just wander in here off the street."

She pulled a can of beer out of the cooler under the bar, set it in front of him, and popped the tab.

"We only serve cans here because these assholes get out of hand, and I don't like cleaning up broken glass."

"There hasn't been a fight with broken glass in almost a year!"

"Jesus, Lance," she said. "I'm surprised you haven't made detective yet. It's been one week shy of a year since I stopped serving anything in glass."

"Oh, right."

"Natty is two bucks," she said.

Dick put a five on the bar and said, "Keep it."

18

"Son of a bitch. You already out tipped all six of these dickheads."

"Comin' in here, throwing' cash around?" Chris said. "You ain't a cop."

"Correct."

"Why are you here?"

"Wanted a beer and I'm meeting someone."

"A cop?"

"A detective."

"Which one?"

"Carland Cooper."

"Ha!" said one of the others. "Good old Coop. Are you one of those A.I.s?"

"A what?" Dick asked.

"Anonymous Informant," he said.

"My god," Pam said. "It's a wonder I sleep at all knowing you fools are out there protecting me. Rod, you need to read a book or watch a cop movie or something. It's C.I., not A.I. Confidential Informant."

"Go easy on him, Pam," Chris said. "One of us has to be the dumb one."

"That title is still up for grabs," she said. "You keep tipping like that, and I'll be happy to do table service."

"It's all good," Dick said. "I don't mind walking over here."

"You expecting him soon?"

"Ten minutes or so."

"Ok," she said and started making a drink. "Here."

"Old Fashioned," Dick said. "That must be his go to drink."

"Has he been drinking somewhere else?" she asked.

"Possibly."

"That mother fucker."

"I think he'll be here more often again pretty soon."

"Five bucks for the drink."

"Here," he said and put a hundred on the bar. "Let me know when I'm out."

"Gladly," she said. "See that boys?"

Dick went back to his chair and put Carl's drink in front of the spot next to him. He took out his phone and googled the address that he had gotten from Olivia. It was for a small, rented office space in a shared working building. The kind of place where there was a lot of traffic, but different people most days. Easy to blend in.

When the door opened again, Dick had to blink a couple times. He could see why they had yelled at him to close the door. This patron knew to shut it immediately. It was Carl.

"Thanks, Pam!" he said when he got to the table. "Put it on my tab."

"He paid for it."

"Thanks, Dick."

"Have a seat, Carl."

"Sure," he said and took off his jacket. He draped it over the back of the seat. "Did you talk to Carla today?"

"No. I don't anticipate needing to talk to her until we figure some things out for you."

"I don't think there is anything to figure out, friend. I've simply lost my touch."

"I don't buy it. Here," Dick said and slid his phone in front of Carl. "What do you think of that office space?"

"I've been there before. Mostly startups or people who want a spot to work that isn't at home."

"What if the person in question wasn't in a startup and had actual offices of their own? Why would they go there?"

"What does this have to do with me?"

"Nothing."

"Then why do I care?"

"I need to see you work."

"I already did my work for today," Carl said and took a drink. "I'm not that interested in doing yours, too."

"Did you break a case today?"

"Don't be a dick."

"I mean…"

"You know what I meant."

Dick sipped at his beer and ran his finger along the rim at the top of the can.

"Alright. If what you said was the situation, then I'd say the guy is doing something on the side. Still needs a place to meet with people that isn't his house or somewhere public. Also, can't meet them at his office. Moonlighting maybe?"

"I'd say that's a good start."

"What else do you know?"

"Not much, yet. Just picked up the case."

"Fine. What else do you want to talk about?" Carl asked. "I'd rather get my drinks from Jen."

"I don't blame you there. Do you work with any of these six guys?"

"Sure. I've worked with all of them at some point."

"They don't seem to be the sharpest knives in the drawer."

"Well, I would say they aren't knives at all. Spoons really. Maybe not good at cutting meat, but they're good at what they do. Except for Lance. That guy's an idiot."

Dick laughed. All six men turned to look.

"Oh, hey, Coop," Chris said. "Didn't see you come in."

"You looked right at me."

"Sun was in my eyes."

"Sure."

"What're you guys talking about? Need some help?"

"We'll figure it out on our own, but thanks."

"Glad to help, Coop."

"Fuck him," Carl said under his breath.

"What?"

"He knows I hate when they call me that."

"Coop?"

"Yeah. That's not my nickname, but these younger guys started calling me that a couple years ago. They wanted to use the name my old partner gave me back when I was in their shoes, but I told them no. They didn't deserve that and I'm not their friend."

"What did your partner call you?"

"Hawk."

"Good name."

"Yeah. He said I had the ability to pick out a detail from a mile like a hawk hunting in a grassy field."

"Where is he now?"

"Francisco? Oh, he's up in Sunset Hill Gardens."

"The cemetery? Sorry to hear that."

"Cancer got him about seven years ago. I don't let anyone call me Hawk anymore. No offense."

"None taken, Carl."

"I guess you are ok with a nickname though."

"Well, we all had one in the service, but I haven't had one since I've been out."

"Dick isn't a nickname?"

"Nope. That's my actual name."

"Your parents had a twisted sense of humor."

"That's one way of putting it," Dick said and took a drink of beer. "Have you worked with any of these guys since things have gone cold?"

"Yeah. Nothing major, though. I can pull up a list of my cases to see who all I've worked with in the last year."

"No, let's just go from memory. I don't want anyone linking me to your cases right now."

"Maybe later, then?"

"I don't like to say something won't happen, but I'd like to stay insulated from your work."

"Probably best," Carl said and finished his drink. "I'm ready, Pam!"

"Alright," she said and went to work on his refill.

"What about the guys playing pool?"

"Detective Poirot is the one in the blue shirt."

"Poirot? Seriously?"

"Well, Adrian Horne, but that ridiculous mustache mixed with the fact that he tells everyone he is half French led us to the nickname. He sees it as an honor."

"The other one? He's a big boy."

"Harry Gold. Sergeant. He could be a detective, but he likes what he does. Probably spends more time at the gym than he does at home. No harm in that, I guess."

"I wouldn't want to tangle with him."

"That's a good plan," Carl said and looked to the bar. Pam held up his fresh drink and then placed it at the end. He retrieved it. "So, what do we do next?"

"Do you have email?"

"Email? Sure. We all have emails assigned to us by the department."

"No, I mean a personal account."

"Nah, I hate that stuff."

"I'll make you a paper copy, then. Carla gave me your address, so I'll send a copy of what I know about the case I want you to assist on by courier in a couple hours."

"Sounds expensive. You can just drop it off."

"I don't want anyone to see me at your house."

"They are seeing us here."

"This is much less risky."

"Is someone watching me?"

"No clue, but we'll find out."

"So, what do you want me to do with the papers when I get them?"

"Read them. Very basic still. Start thinking about possibilities. I'll meet you for coffee at the little shop in that workspace. It looks like they have several open working areas that you are supposed to pay to use, so I'll get one that is close to the guy we're going to watch."

"Sounds easy enough. I do have to work, though. Even if I'm not solving anything, I have to put in the hours."

"It'll be fine," Dick said. "Bring stuff with you if you want. Definitely going to be some waiting involved. He might not show up at all."

"I can do maybe two hours in the morning."

"That's a good start. Do me a favor and make sure you don't say anything about it to people at work. Definitely don't put anything on your work computer."

"Wouldn't dream of it. I still don't know what we're doing exactly."

"Proving that you aren't the defective detective."

"Using my words against me?"

"Just tying them in."

"Nice touch. I take it you aren't staying for another?"

"I've got to handle some other business. We can meet up at ten in the morning."

"Going down to see Jen, I suppose?"

"Not tonight. I really do have work to do."

"Well, I'm done for today. I guess I'll just have a few more of these."

"Pam?" Dick asked, turning to look at the bartender.

"Yeah?"

"Keep a third of that cash for yourself and get Detective Cooper whatever he wants with the rest. If he doesn't drink it, then you can keep that, too."

"You're welcome back anytime," she said. "Didn't catch your name."

"Probably better that way," Dick said and went out the door.

"I really think he is one of the Anonymous Informants," Rod said.

"You're hopeless," Pam said before grabbing a rag to start wiping down the bar.

3

A three-story parking garage served The Commons, which was the shared working space where Jack Nelson had rented an office. In back of that was an asphalt parking lot. Dick used that open lot instead of testing the height bar at the entrance to the garage. This gave him access from the alley behind the complex, which allowed him to stay off the cameras that tracked everyone using the garage.

He parked his truck in the back row. The limbs of a poorly trimmed oak tree provided a little shade, although it was a pleasant temperature that morning. He brought a laptop case with him, but the laptop itself was one he had picked up at a pawn shop and held nothing of value.

A sidewalk ran along one end of the garage between two rows of shrubs that were about a foot tall. Everything was well manicured, which seemed normal for high dollar spaces like this. Dick glanced into the garage to see two men in suits talking and a completely full first floor. Nothing of interest there.

A concrete ramp wound up and around a fountain on the way to the back entrance. The water sprayed up about twenty feet. The mist coming off of it fell just short of the concrete. Dick elected to use the stairs. The tap on the steps from his brown Santoni dress shoes was the only sound other than the gently falling water.

"Good morning, sir. Welcome to The Commons," said a woman at a desk a few steps inside the door. "Can I help you find an office or common area today?"

"I'm meeting someone at the coffee shop you have here. Can you point me in the right direction?" he asked, appreciating her alert hazel eyes and flawless brown skin.

"I'm engaged," she said.

"Congratulations."

"I could see it in your eyes."

"Can't blame me for admiring."

"I suppose not. The coffee shop is on the second floor near the north end. The elevators are over there, but the open staircase at the center of the floor is faster."

"The stairs it is. Thank you."

"I do have to get your name, for security purposes."

"Sure. It's Dick Wondercock."

"Now that's the most ridiculous thing I've heard in a while," she said, fighting back a smile.

Dick took out his credentials and showed them to her. She shook her head and typed his name onto a spreadsheet.

"You win," she said.

"I haven't won anything yet. See you on the way out."

"Everyone should have a dream."

Dick winked and tucked away his private investigator identification. He turned for the stairs and didn't look back as he walked over to them. He could feel her watching him walk away.

"Probably what they feel when I watch them go," he said to himself.

A younger man in a plain, black t-shirt and jeans raced past him on the stairs. Dick paused for a moment to watch him go on ahead. He began to wonder what kind of people work in this mixed environment.

When he reached the top of the stairs, he glanced to his right and saw the coffee shop. There were two rows of tables and several small groupings of oversized leather chairs. Each group had a round coffee table in its center. There were people in most of the chairs, but only four tables were occupied. He went on to the shop.

"What can we make for you today?" asked the man at the counter. Dick realized it was the same person who had run past him on the stairs.

"I'll just take a black coffee."

"What size?"

"Large is good. Do you offer refills?"

"The bottomless cup is a dollar extra."

"Give me that."

"Cup or mug?"

"What's the difference?"

"The cups are the paper option. The mugs are reusable. It's the eco-friendly choice."

"I see," Dick said. "I guess a mug will work."

"Good choice," the worker said. "Anything to eat?"

"Not right now."

"Very good. That'll be four twenty-five."

Dick smiled and took out his wallet. He found a five-dollar bill and handed it to the man. Another worker, a woman in her thirties, put the mug on the counter in front of him and went back to the next order.

"Seventy-five cents is your change. Enjoy your drink," the worker said. "Come back up when you're ready for a refill."

"Will do," Dick said and dropped the coins in the tip jar.

He saw an empty group of chairs to the left of the tables. That seemed like a good place to talk with Carl. The tables looked too formal anyway.

It was the second grouping from the coffee shop. He selected the chair with its back to the large plants forming a ring around the seating area. Taking a look at his phone, he saw he was ten minutes early and had two emails waiting.

Sipping from the mug in his left hand, he started reading the first email. It was from a friend and fellow private investigator, Sebastien Byrd, who was halfway across the country. He needed some first-hand intel on a person of interest and hoped Dick would help him out. He typed a quick response telling him to send the information.

Then, he took a couple drinks while looking around the seating area. Almost everyone was on a laptop or phone. He didn't see Jack Nelson. He also didn't see Carl, but he still had six minutes to spare. A strange smell caught his attention, so he turned to look at the large plants behind him. They were peace lilies, but he was sure they shouldn't smell like that. He leaned over to see a used diaper with dinosaurs on it. He moved to a different table.

The second email took a little longer to get through. It was from a potential client, Donald Mueller, who owned a massive record collection, but believed someone had been stealing his vinyl over the last year. He gave the information about what the police had found. The case had stalled, and he didn't know what to do next. The idea of losing more records left him unable to sleep. Dick felt like that would be outside his normal realm of work, however he decided to tell Donald that he would meet with him in a few days.

He sent the response and put his phone away. The coffee was still steaming. He finished the cup and went to get a refill. The worker recognized him, took the cup, filled it, and gave it back. No words were exchanged. Only a polite smile came with the coffee.

Dick looked up at a large analog clock on the wall. It was two minutes after nine. Carl was late, which seemed odd. He weaved through the growing crowd of people and made his way back to the seating area. Carl was there. He was in the chair to the left of the one Dick had been using.

"You don't seem like the kind of guy to be late for appointments," Dick said, retaking his chair.

"I wasn't late."

"Right on time, then."

"No, I've been here for about an hour. I was sitting over there," Carl said and pointed to a couch that was outside a pair of offices. "I saw you come up the stairs, get coffee, and start working on your phone."

"Why?"

"You brought me here to see how I work. I wanted the chance to see how you acted when you didn't know I was here."

"And?"

"Pretty boring. I thought you'd see me when you came in, but I could tell your mind was elsewhere. Was it the woman working the desk downstairs or the kid who ran past you on the stairs?"

"A little of both maybe."

"Makes sense. I will say that I rarely set an appointment with someone where I can't scope out the situation ahead of time."

"You didn't check out the Ironclad ahead of time."

"No need. That place hasn't changed in at least twenty years. Also, there is little to no risk of something going wrong there. This place is loaded with variables that are way out of my control."

"Good point."

"I haven't seen anyone matching the picture of John Nelson, Jr. that you sent me. I did locate his office, but there isn't much to see there. Looks to be two or three rooms. I couldn't tell the exact layout. The front room is a desk and a chair with some fake plants. Got the feeling it hadn't been used in a while."

"That doesn't make me feel good about seeing him today."

"Well, we might not see him here, but I'm sure you can find him."

"Probably true."

"So, what do you want to see me do? Watching me work is not something I've had someone do since I was brand new."

"Talk me through the information I sent you and then let's come up with a plan. You said you only have a couple hours this morning."

"Right. Gotta do my actual job or at least try to do it."

"We're going to figure that out next."

"I appreciate the confidence, but I don't think there is anything to figure out. I'm just getting too old for this."

"We'll see. Now, start talking."

"Fine," Carl said and flipped open the folder in front of him. "Due to the public nature of this spot, I'll call him Mr. X."

"Creative."

"Mr. X is married with three kids. Next month will be his seventeenth anniversary. His kids are ages 15, 13, and 4."

"Oops."

"Yeah. He is one of the junior partners of a private equity firm owned by his grandfather and run by his father, we'll call him Mr. X, Sr., and his uncle, Thomas. He has a brother and four cousins who are also junior partners. The slices of the pie are getting smaller."

Dick kept working on his coffee.

"His salary plus bonuses put him in the six-figure range, but he's never gone over two hundred thousand. That leads us to what you were hoping to find."

"Hoping to find? I'm confident that there is more to Mr. X than we already know. He's got a storage unit linked to the office here. Neither one is in his legal name."

"I noticed that. JNJ Investments isn't a very creative name if he's trying to hide something. However, there aren't any links between JNJ and the family business."

"None?"

"Nothing I found. I even tried to find out if JNJ had invested in anything that Grandpa's business was managing. Insider trading and all that."

"That would make sense. Maybe Mr. X is smarter than we think."

"It does seem that way. What else do we know?"

"That's pretty much it. Does he have hobbies?"

"I had roughly fourteen hours to do this research. I also managed to get some sleep in there because I think this is a waste of time."

"I see," Dick said. "So, I need to figure out what JNJ is actually doing."

"One of us does. I'm not sure what your timeline is, but I don't have a lot of extra time right now. Moonlighting isn't popular among my leadership."

"Got it. I think we're close."

"Maybe we need to find him and ask him directly. If someone is on his tail, it is possible he'll give up the information."

"I'll try to track him down and set up something," Dick said.

"I have a sneaking suspicion that this is being blown way out of proportion."

"Perhaps."

"Can I ask who wants to know what is going on with JNJ?"

"I think that's a good question. Let me see what I can find out tomorrow."

"You don't know who is asking?"

"I do. In fact, that's who is paying the bills right now. I just want to see how that revelation will affect your research on this."

"What bills? Carla is paying you to talk to me and someone else is paying you to figure out JNJ. Sounds like you're winning all around."

"Yes," Dick said. "I can see how you'd come to that conclusion. I am crossing streams on this, so to speak. Introducing risk into situations where there wasn't any before is a special task."

"So, what do you want to see? I'm assuming you'll come out of this ok financially."

"That is yet to be determined."

"Ok. Do you know what's in the storage unit?"

"I don't."

"But you know the unit is linked to this office?"

"Yes. It is registered to the office here."

"How did you learn that?"

"I made an exchange."

"You paid the manager off?"

"Not exactly."

"So, I have one more thing," Carl said. "I did a couple searches and found that the business has assets."

"Do tell."

"JNJ Investments holds the deeds on five rental properties. All single-family occupancy. JNJ also owns a 2008 Chevy Express 1500 Cargo Van."

"What color is it?"

"White."

"Of course it is."

"Getting back to the properties," Carl said. "Owning those seems like a stretch from an equity fund."

"True," Dick said. "There is definitely more to be figured out here. What's in the storage unit? What else is JNJ being used for? We need to find Jack Nelson."

"I think so. Wait, have you been to his house?"

"No. I did check out his neighborhood on Google."

"I bet he's keeping the van at the storage unit," Carl said. "Betting his HOA doesn't allow commercial vehicles to be sitting around. Can your helper at the storage place get us surveillance video?"

"Probably. Let's go see if he's at the office now."

They both gathered their things and stood. Dick led the way out of the seating area and along one side of the arched common area toward the office. When they got there, they found it still dark.

"I'm guessing he only comes here for appointments," Carl said.

"Makes sense," Dick said and moved closer to the office's single large window. It had a lone piece of paper taped to the inside with a color photo of a small house. "For rent. Immediate availability. Students welcome."

"That number doesn't match what I have for his home or cell."

"Call it. Let's get him to meet us there."

"Good idea," Carl said, pulling his phone from his shirt pocket.

"No," Dick said. "Don't use your department phone."

"It shows as unavailable on caller ID."

"Here," he said and dug into his inside coat pocket. "Burner phone. He can see it's a real number at least."

"Never had to worry about that."

"Trust me on this one."

"Fine," Carl said. He powered on the phone, typed in the number, and hit send.

It rang four times. Carl thought it was going to go to voicemail, but instead a man answered.

"JNJ."

"Uh, yeah, I'm calling about the house you have for rent."

"Sure. The one on Felipe?"

"Yes. What's the rent?"

"900 a month. Deposit of 500, first and last month's rent due when you move in."

"Sounds good. Can I see it today?"

"Sorry, no. I'm booked today. I am showing it at noon and one tomorrow. Could you be there at two?"

"I can do that," Carl said, getting into the scenario.

"Are you a student?"

"I'm not. Is that a requirement?"

"Not at all. Just want you to be aware that there are several houses in that area with university students and it can get loud at times."

"No worries."

"Caller ID says you're from out of the area?"

"New to town. Haven't gotten a local number yet."

"That doesn't matter. Just wondering."

"Ok."

"What's your name?"

"Carl."

"See you at two tomorrow, Carl. I'm Jack."

"Thanks."

The call ended and Dick gave him a thumbs up.

"I guess you heard all that?"

"Sure did. Bold of you to use your real name."

"What name should I have used?"

"Totally up to you, but a little anonymity can go a long way in this line of work."

"I hope I'm not in this line of work much longer. Tomorrow is about the end of involvement in this."

"Agreed. I'll have what I need by the end of that visit."

"What is it that you need?"

"You'll see."

"This isn't a hit or something, is it?"

"No, but I guess I'd say no either way."

"True."

"Well, give me the benefit of the doubt on this one. Carla did find me as a private investigator, not as an assassin.

"I'll go with that for now."

"Want to meet for lunch tomorrow?"

"I have to get some work done tomorrow, but I know there is a little diner called Henry's near the house Jack is going to show us. I can be there around one thirty."

"That'll do. I'll see you tomorrow."

Carl nodded, looked toward the stairs, and decided to go to the elevator instead. Dick watched him go but wanted to take the stairs. He needed to talk to the woman at the desk one more time.

4

Dick pulled his truck into the last spot in front of Henry's Diner at a quarter after one the next day. It was a throwback with a chrome facade and large plate glass windows. It was situated along one of the feeder streets leading up into the neighborhood where Jack's house was.

The building sat parallel with the hill, so he could see into the windows easier with each step as he approached the front door. He fully expected to find Carl waiting for him, but he wasn't there. Instead, he noticed that only two booths were occupied and one man in a suit sat at the counter.

"Sit anywhere you like," said a woman in a retro waitress outfit from behind the Formica top. She had sandy blonde hair wrapped into a tight bun pinned to the top of her head.

"Thanks," he said and walked along the row of booths to the very last one. He sat facing the door. The tabletop matched the counter, and everything looked surprisingly clean for as old as this place had to be.

He took a laminated sheet of paper serving as the menu from a silver stand near the window. He debated the all-day breakfast. Bacon and eggs were good for any meal in his opinion. Ultimately, he went with his standard option.

"Hey, honey. I'm Linda. What can I get for you today?"

"Well, Linda, I think I'll go with a cheeseburger and some fries."

"One or two patties?"

"One is fine. Do you have cheddar?"

"American."

"Ok."

"What to drink?"

"Pepsi?"

"We got Coke products."

"Coke is fine."

"Anything else?"

"That'll be enough."

"All right," she said and went back behind the counter. There was a silver wheel of sorts hanging from the top of the pass-through window. She stuck his ticket under one of the small springs and gave it a half turn. Dick saw a thick hand at the end of a hairy arm grab it.

"Can't get more stereotypical than this," he said and took out his phone. He had a text from Olivia. It was only a picture and he tried to figure out how she got the camera into that angle. No other communication was waiting on him. He decided to take in the scenery instead of messing around on his phone.

The man in the suit at the counter was sipping some coffee while picking at a piece of pie. The couple at the far end of the room were in a booth perpendicular to his, so he got a good look at them. He figured they were in their sixties. They were having a quiet conversation. She was eating a club sandwich. He had a salad.

The other couple was two booths from him. It didn't appear they had their food yet and they weren't talking. The woman was facing him, and the man was looking out the window. She had wavy red hair. After a few moments, she looked over the man's shoulder to make eye contact with Dick. He smiled and she shifted her gaze.

"Food'll be out in a couple minutes," Linda said to the couple.

"Thanks," the man said.

Dick turned his attention outside, where Carl had just pulled up. He stepped out of his car, slammed the door, and started pacing along the street. He was yelling into his phone, but Dick couldn't tell what he was saying.

After a few seconds, Carl poked the phone with his finger. He jammed it back in his pocket and turned to face away from the diner. He stared at the house across the street for almost a minute before taking off his hat and throwing it to the ground. He stomped on it and then kicked it out into the road. A car swerved but failed to miss it. Dick saw Carl's shoulders slump as he walked out into the street to retrieve his ruined fedora.

He walked back toward the diner, trying to reshape the hat while knocking off filth from the road. He stopped near the driver's door of his car. He yelled something in frustration, yanked open the door, and threw in the hat. He slammed the door again.

He straightened himself and his jacket. He ran his fingers over his hair and took a deep breath. Then, he looked up to see the patrons staring back at him. Dick tipped his Coke to him. Carl shook his head and climbed the stairs to the entrance. No one said anything to him as he walked back to Dick's booth and slid in to face him.

"Bad day at the office?"

"God damn fucking right it is."

"Wow, Carl. Want to talk about it?"

"Sir, what can I get you to drink?" Linda said, easing up to the table.

"Coffee. Black."

"Anything to eat?"

"No."

"Be right back," she said.

"Three weeks. Three fucking weeks to get a new number on a guy I've been trying to track down for a year. About an hour ago, the number showed disconnected. This is the shit that makes me crazy. I'm doing something wrong here! Might as well give Carla her money back. I'll pay for whatever the bill is up to."

"First of all, you don't know that the number change had anything to do with you."

"Yes, I..."

"Shut the fuck up, Carl," Dick said, staring him straight in the eyes. "Let me talk."

"Fine."

"We probably shouldn't talk about this here. So, after we're done with our stop, we'll find somewhere secure to chat."

"You trying to get me to take you to the station again?"

"Not yet. Now, we need to focus on JNJ."

"How am I supposed to do that? My career just keeps disintegrating around me."

"Here's your coffee," Linda said, putting a cup and saucer in front of Carl. "Your cheeseburger will be up in a second. He made a fresh batch of fries."

"Excellent," Dick said. "Can you ask him to put a little extra salt on them?"

"Sure thing."

"Thank you, Linda," he said and offered a wink. She blushed and went to the pass-through.

"Do you flirt with everyone?"

"No. I'm just being nice."

"I bet."

"You're just upset I haven't flirted with you."

"Jesus…"

Dick smiled and took a drink of Coke. Linda returned with a platter. The fries were still steaming, and he could see the salt on them.

"Can I get you a refill?"

"That'd be great."

Linda took his glass and went to the fountain.

"What's the plan for JNJ? Do you want me to actually rent the place?"

"No. Don't be silly."

"I don't know where the end of this thing is. I've got actual work to do."

"Look, I know you're pissed about this phone number and whatever else has gone wrong. We're going to figure that out next. I need you to see this thing with Jack through to the end, ok? This is the last stop, but you can't go in all upset. Got it?"

39

"Fuck," Carl said and took a drink of coffee. "Fine. I'll help you with Jack and then I'm out. You can move on to your next case or whatever."

"No, I still have work to do with you. After your research on Jack, I'm confident that your approach isn't the problem. I'm going to become your shadow. You're so close to your daily routines that you might be missing something. Fresh eyes, you know?"

"A babysitter."

"A helper. I'm not going to keep you out of trouble. Just offering insight," Dick said. "Now, I'm going to eat before these fantastic looking fries cool off completely. You do some deep thinking or whatever to get your shit together before we go to the house."

Carl didn't say anything. He looked out the window and worked on his coffee. Linda swung by with the pot to give a refill twice before Dick finished his lunch. It was twenty minutes until the appointment.

"Better now?" Dick asked.

"Sure."

"Good. We're going to ride up together in my truck because your car looks like a cop car."

"It is a cop car."

"Exactly. I'm just a friend you brought along to have a look."

"A friend? He's going to think we're gay."

"You wish," Dick said.

"I'm too old for this shit."

"All right. I'll drive up there and you do the talking. Just find out the basics, have a look around, and then tell him you'd like to step outside to talk to me for a minute. Throw in something about really liking it or whatever."

"Fine."

"Have another cup. We've got plenty of time."

"I'm going to piss my pants if I drink anymore."

"Linda, do you have a bathroom?"

"God damn it," Carl mumbled.

"Other end of the counter, through that plain white door."

Carl slid out and handled his business. He came back to a fresh cup of coffee. Dick's plate was gone, but he was sipping at his Coke.

"Better?"

"I'm not five."

"I'm well aware. I paid the bill, but feel free to finish your cup."

"Thanks so much."

"You're welcome," Dick said and looked over Carl's shoulder.

The woman with the red hair was alone at the booth now. The man that was with her had gone into the bathroom. She didn't look away this time and he got a good look at her green eyes. There was mutual interest, but he couldn't think of a way to make the connection.

"I'm ready when you are," Carl said, putting down his empty cup.

"Yep, let's go."

They both slid out of their seats and straightened their jackets. The man was coming back. Carl moved past him, but Dick paused to let him take his seat. He used that moment to look at the woman one last time. She looked disappointed and he was sure he did, too.

"Let's go loverboy," Carl said from the passenger side of Dick's truck.

"Loverboy?"

"I saw the way she was looking at you. Don't have to be a detective to pick up on that. I'm surprised that guy didn't sock you."

"Sock me? What year is this, Carl?"

"Unlock the door."

41

They got in. Dick backed out and turned the truck up the hill. His GPS had him turn left, go three blocks, and then turn right. It was the fourth house on the left. One of several similar homes in that block. Dick parked on the street across from it. They were five minutes early, but it looked like the previous potential tenant was already gone. Only a white Chevy van was in front of the house.

"Show time," Dick said.

"Who's the guy in the Cadillac?" Carl asked, noticing a spotless, white sedan a few houses away.

"No idea."

"Doesn't fit the neighborhood."

"Let's focus on Jack."

"Fine. I still don't understand why we are going through with this. You wanted to watch me do my thing and I did it. Talking to him seems unnecessary."

"Gotta make sure it's him."

"Who else would it be?"

"We're already here. Let's just go in."

"Fine," Carl said and opened his door. He got out and walked around the front of the truck, where Dick was waiting.

"You go first."

Carl checked for traffic and gave the Cadillac another glance. He took the concrete stairs from the street up to the sidewalk and then to the front door. The front door was open, so he knocked on the frame and went in.

"Hey! Welcome!" said a man coming from the hallway into the living room. "I'm Jack."

"Carl."

"And your friend?"

"I'm Richard," Dick said. Carl smirked.

"Well, let's have a look around. Feel free to ask questions along the way."

"Ok."

"So, this is the living room. Hardwood floors through the house. Good natural light."

"That'll be good for your plants, Carl," Dick said.

"Yeah."

They went on to the kitchen, which was directly behind the living room. Then, they came back through to the hallway. He showed them the bedrooms and a small bathroom that had purple and gray tiles, something straight out of the sixties.

"That's pretty much it. There is a basement. You can get to it from the kitchen. It's not a livable space and is more like a cellar. It does get wet in heavy rain, so don't store anything in cardboard down there. Probably best to keep it off the ground. Any questions?"

"You said you had other showings?" Carl asked.

"Yes. I've done a few. Probably hear back from one of them today or tomorrow. This neighborhood is in demand."

"Ok, well, I like it. Do you mind if Richard and I step outside to talk for a minute?"

"Sure thing. I have one more showing in about an hour. If you decide to take it, I'll cancel that one."

"Good deal. Thank you," Carl said and went to the front door. "Let's go, Richard."

Dick followed him outside and down to the sidewalk. Carl stood with his back to the door so that Jack wouldn't be able to tell what he was saying, if he was even watching.

"So, what do you think? Ready to move in?" Dick asked.

"Look. I did everything you asked, and this still feels fishy. What's the next step? I need to get back to work."

"Your part is done," Dick said and gave a quick wave of his right hand toward the Cadillac."

"God damn it. Is this a sting? I can't be part of anything like that."

"No. Not at all. You can wait in the truck, if you want."

"I'm staying. I need to know what you've implicated me in."

"Implicated. You're a funny man."

The man from the car strode up the stairs and stopped next to Dick. He was wearing an expensive suit. His hair was mostly gray, but a few dark brown strands could still be seen. His smile was perfect.

"Mr. Nelson," Dick said, shaking hands with the man.

"Mr. Wondercock. I have to admit that your name is odd, but it's good to meet you in person. Please call me John, though."

"You'll never forget my name at least. Good advertising. And if we're using first names, you can call me Dick."

"I suppose it would be a hard name to forget. Anyway, I do appreciate you figuring this out for me."

"Absolutely. Hope it was worth the fee."

"It was. Is this your assistant?"

"Not really. This is Carl Cooper. He helped me out on this, but it was a one-time thing."

"Detective Carl Cooper," he said and shook the man's hand.

"Ah," John said. "Did Jack do something illegal?"

"Not at all. Everything he has done is by the book, as far as I can see. Can't really go into the work I'm doing with Detective Cooper."

"Understood. So, what do we do next?"

"Dad?" Jack asked from the front door.

"Hi, Son."

"Why are you here?" Jack asked, walking down the stairs. "Do you know these men?"

"One of them, yes. I had Dick figuring out where you go when you leave the office during the day."

"You had me followed?"

"Sort of. I asked you several times and you always had an excuse."

"Jesus. I'm a grown man."

"Yes. Yes. So, what is this house?"

44

"It's a house. These two were talking about renting it. I guess that was all made up."

"My apologies," Dick said. "Part of the process."

"What process?"

"Look, Jack, I just needed to talk to you about this. Why are you showing a rental property to people? It's yours?"

"Yes, Dad. I own a few houses. Mostly fixer-uppers that I buy on the cheap and do repairs."

"Sounds expensive."

"Not at all. I do the work myself."

"You do the work? How do you know how to do that stuff? I don't even know how to do that."

Jack sighed and said, "I like it. I started doing work on my house about ten years ago. It was fun to work with my hands and a big switch from my regular job."

"So, it's a hobby?"

"It's an investment. A profitable one at that."

"What about the family business?"

"Dad, I don't know how to tell you this, but I hate it. It's boring."

John laughed and said, "Really?"

"Yes."

"Well, you are right about that. It is extremely boring."

"So why do you keep doing it?"

"It's what I'm expected to do! Your grandpa has his plans and that's all that matters."

"And it's what I'm expected to do."

"What? By who?"

"What do you mean?"

"I mean that I thought you liked it. It does pay well."

"Sure. Kelly, the kids, and I are all comfortable. I'm not quitting anytime soon. Definitely can't pay the bills on the rent from these houses."

"I tell you what. I'll make you an offer. You think on it and get back to me."

"Ok."

"What if I buy out what would have been your share of the company eventually? You use that money to buy more houses."

"My share won't be that much, and you aren't going anywhere for a while."

"I'm not going to work until I'm my dad's age. No way. Still, the company will be worth a lot by the time your generation takes over."

"How much are you talking about? I can just keep working for the business and build these houses up. I can add one every other year or so."

"Three million seems fair."

"What?" Jack said. "I can't take three million from you."

"You can if I'm buying something from you. I thought about it when Dick told me that you owned properties. Now, I know why, and I want to make sure you get to enjoy yourself."

"I need to talk to Kelly. This is big."

"Good. Call her. You can keep working until you're ready, if you decide to accept the offer. I'm sure it'll take a while to get houses bought, fixed up, and rented."

"I don't know what to say."

"Ok, well, call me tomorrow. I'm going to get back to work."

"I'll be there in a couple hours."

"Nah. Finish up whatever you need to do here and go home. Talk to Kelly."

"Alright."

"Good," John said. "Dick, I assume you received the remainder of the money?"

"I did. Thank you."

"Detective Cooper, it was nice to meet you."

"Likewise."

"Bye, Jack."

"Bye, Dad."

Dick and Carl went back to the truck. Dick started it up and went on up the block to find a cross street to turn around on.

"Do I get a cut of that or what?" Carl asked.

"No, but I'll buy you a drink."

"Seems a little skewed in your favor."

"Maybe. Depends on how your case turns out."

"What exactly is my case and what is the next step in your opinion?"

"Your case is figuring out what's going wrong."

"I've lost my touch. Not much of a case there."

"No, that's not it."

"You think you know that just because we found Jack Nelson?"

"No, but you haven't lost anything. I want to take a couple hours to think on this. Can I talk you into meeting up at Harry's later tonight?"

"That's the first suggestion you've made that I'm on board with."

"I'll meet you there about eight," Dick said, pulling in behind Carl's sedan at the diner.

"I'll probably be there around seven."

"I might be able to make that but try not to get too hammered before we talk."

"I don't work for you," Carl said and got out of the truck.

5

"Fuuuuck," Jen screamed out in ecstasy. She looked down into Dick's eyes and felt him give a little thrust. "You can finish now."

"Oh, I've been done for a few minutes already."

"Seriously?"

"Yeah," he said and pulled her down into his embrace. He hugged her tight while keeping himself firmly inside her. "Stay just like that."

"How did you stay hard so long?"

"Practice," he said. "Let's just enjoy this a little longer. No one is knocking on the door this time."

"So true. Laura is a bit of a buzzkill."

"Just don't get too used to this."

"I know," she said. "We won't be together forever."

"It's not personal."

"I know. Too many ladies, too little time."

"That's not it at all."

"It kinda is."

"Hey," he said, taking her gently by both sides of the head with his hands. "I really like you, but the way I get by is not good for a relationship."

"I've heard about Dick Wondercock. It's ok. I'm enjoying what I get."

"Ok," he said and flipped her over in a quick motion. He was still inside her and looking down into her wide eyes. "I'm not over this and I hope you aren't either."

"I'll never be over it."

"Yes. You will be someday."

"Seems unlikely. I'm enjoying myself too much."

"Yeah, well, once I have to scoot off to work one too many times, you'll draw the line and that will be the end of it."

"I'm a patient woman."

"I'm sure you are," he said and rolled off to his left. "This isn't on you. I promise."

"Ok."

"I have to go to Harry's in a little bit."

"To see Laura?"

"No. That's not something that will ever happen."

"Why not? She's beautiful."

"Maybe so, but I'm going there for business. I have to talk to a client."

"Ok. Will you come back later?"

"I probably shouldn't. Tomorrow is a big day. If I come back here, I won't get any sleep."

"That's true. Will you call me though?"

"You know I will."

"Sounds like something from a Lifetime Christmas movie."

"Nah. I'm not wholesome enough for one of those," Dick said.

"Me neither."

"You could be," he said and slid to the edge of the bed to pull on his boxers.

"One more go?"

"Not right now, but I'll be back soon enough."

"An empty promise, I bet."

"You'll have to trust me," he said and got to his feet. He pulled on a t-shirt and his pants. Then, his button up shirt followed by his socks and shoes. "I like you a lot."

"I like you, too."

"Good. I'm going to be tied up for the next couple days, but we can catch a movie or dinner or something this weekend if you want."

"I'd be ok with that," she said.

"It's a date. Now, I have to take off."

"Are you sure?"

"Yes. Work to do."

"Ok," she said.

He gave her a kiss on the forehead and walked to the front door. He twisted the lock on the knob to the locked position. It latched behind him when he headed for his truck. The sun was setting. His truck started up and the headlights came on. He thought for a moment about going back inside, but that wasn't how he worked.

Dick found a parking spot a half block away from Harry's, which was a near miracle. His truck was not the vehicle they had in mind when they designed the spaces. He locked the doors and took a good look around. He had made some calls about the case with Carl and knew he might start drawing attention.

He didn't see anyone out of the ordinary, but he'd keep his alert up. He looked into the bar on his way to the door, spotting Carl in the same corner booth as last time. There was a chime when he opened the door.

"Welcome to Harry's," a waitress said, approaching him. She had straight, black hair and purple glasses. It looked like she was at least part Vietnamese. "I'm Linh. Just you tonight?"

"I'm meeting the gentleman in the back corner," Dick said, looking Carl's way.

"Do you need a menu?"

"No. I'll take a Jack and Coke. Open a tab for me and put his tab on mine. Also, anything else he orders should go on mine, but don't tell him."

"You sure? He can run up a pretty good bill."

"I'm sure," Dick said and started toward the booth. He looked over to the bar to see a male bartender. That was a first for any of his visits to Harry's.

"You made it," Carl said.

"Three minutes early. Mind if I sit?"

"Are you going to sit anyway?"

"No. If you don't want to do this tonight, I understand. We can wait a day or two."

"Sit down."

"I picked up that you were a little pissed when I dropped you off at the diner."

"A regular Sherlock."

"Look. I needed to see how you worked and it wouldn't have been the same if I created something fake," Dick said.

"It wasn't a difficult case, though."

"Ok, so you said you haven't solved anything in about a year?"

"Right."

"Have they all been hard cases?"

"I guess not."

"Ok, so you see why I did it?"

"A little more knowledge would have been good."

"I didn't want to skew your thoughts. From this point on, I'll share everything."

"Sure," Carl said and finished off his drink. He raised it to draw Linh's attention. "Can I get another?"

"Be right there," she said. She was in the middle of clearing a high-top table.

"So," Carl said to Dick, "what's the next step in the case of me?"

"We need to figure out the big question."

"Which is?"

"Who benefits from you not solving cases?"

"In what way?"

"Financially. That's the big one. There might be other little bonuses for people, but money is the big driver in my experience."

"I suppose so."

Linh walked up, set down Carl's drink, and took his empty.

"Anything else? An appetizer maybe?"

"No thanks," Carl said.

"Ok. Just let me know if you change your mind."

"Will do," he said, and she turned away.

"You want to get into this here or should we look for something more private?"

"We should be good here," Carl said, looking around. "Two booths either way are empty and there's no one at the high tops yet."

"How many cases have you been assigned in the last year?" Dick asked, taking a tablet from his briefcase and powering it up.

"Probably a dozen. When I hit the cold streak, they stopped giving me new ones. I usually do at least forty in a year."

"Are they all related?"

"What? Why would they be related? That'd be a major crimes scenario."

"Look, Carl, I'm trying to figure this thing out."

"Fine. No, they aren't related. Well, if they are related, then I messed up worse than I thought."

"I doubt that. Do you have them memorized?"

"Do you memorize your cases?"

"No, but you don't have any case files with you. Makes it hard to discuss."

"We don't really have physical files anymore. I wish we did. I hate the fucking system they have us using."

"How do you access it?"

"The computer on my desk. That's the only place I deal with it. Some of the detectives have laptops or whatever, but I don't have any interest in taking it home with me. If we are out of the station, we have to use something called a VPN. It's a pain in the ass."

"Not a bad plan. Let's just see what you can remember. Throw one out there. Maybe the oldest from this year?"

"Uh, let's see. That might be the video game system thefts."

"I'm listening."

"Basically, we had reports from about ten different resale stores that had video game stuff go missing. It wasn't just one kind. Nintendo, Xbox, and PlayStation mostly, though. Some games, but usually only the ones that were bundled with a system."

"Not new devices?"

"Only one was new, I think. Anyway, I checked with a few dozen pawn shops in the area. No significant uptick in people wanting to sell. No common suspects showing up at multiple places either. They share a pretty good database between shops for people that are suspected of illegal activity."

"So what do you think they were doing with them?"

"The old days of needing a local outlet to get money for stolen stuff is over. They clean it up really good and throw it online. Facebook Marketplace or eBay are the most common outlets. A couple guys got caught because when one person sells too much, it draws attention. Now, they create another free email address with a new name and set up another account. It costs nothing to do it and keeps them from being watched."

"That's smart."

"Sure is. I had feelers out with a couple video game resale places, but they didn't get hit."

"So that case dried up?"

"Not exactly. Six more shops a little further west lost merchandise. We got no information from those places that helped."

"Maybe the plan you put in place with the targeted shops got shared through that database you talked about?"

"Maybe. It's frustrating though."

"I'm sure. Give me another case."

"Ok," Carl said and put away half his drink. "There are a lot of flea markets around the city, right?"

"Sure."

"I had reports of a trio of people, two men and a woman, who would go through the store very meticulously. They focused on booths with a lot of collectibles. The catch was that the video never got a good look at their face and there was never video of them taking anything. Sure, they picked up a lot of stuff. Most of the time they would look up pieces on their phones and then put them back."

"Researching collectibles isn't illegal."

"Obviously. The problem came when the people who owned the stuff in the booths started making claims to the flea market owners that some of their collectibles were fake. However, they weren't when they put them in the booth."

"Hard to prove that."

"Yeah, it is, but when there are claims by that many people in that many different locations, it warrants an investigation. We eventually came up with names for two of them."

"Oh yeah?"

"When I got the judge to sign off on my search request for those two, they had nothing in their house that tied them to any of the fake items. Not a single thing. The judge wasn't very happy with me. We kept an eye on those two over the next three months and they did nothing wrong. They still went to flea markets, but there were no more claims of fake collectibles."

"Damn."

"You're telling me. Hey, look, Laura's here," Carl said and waved to her.

"Hello, Carl. Dick."

"Hi, Laura," Carl said. "Working a later shift tonight?"

"Had to meet with the owners. That's why Charlie is working the bar. Had to make him stay over from the day shift."

"Jen's not working tonight?" Dick asked her.

"I think you know the answer to that," she said, rolling her eyes. "We talk."

"Ah."

"Anyway, I have to get Charlie out of here. You two ready for another?"

"I am," Carl said, finishing his old fashioned.

"I'm ok."

"I'll send Linh over with a refill, Carl."

"Thanks, Laura. You're the best."

"You are," she said and gave him a wink. She walked to the little hallway that led to her office.

"You old flirt," Dick said.

"You don't get to judge me, but maybe I am. I'm not quite dead yet."

"Hey, I don't blame you."

"So where's Jen?"

"She's off tonight."

"But she said you know where she is?"

"Yeah, well, let's focus on this case."

"What happened to transparency?"

"Jen's location is not pertinent to this case, but she's at home."

"And you know that because?"

"You're the detective. Draw a conclusion."

"Got it. You sly dog."

"Seriously, though, give me one more. Maybe something more recent?"

"Let's see," Carl said as Linh showed up with his drink. She smiled and set it on his napkin but didn't say anything. "There's a recurring group of thefts happening at big box stores. Mostly tools at Lowe's and Home Depot and small electronics at Walmart and Target. I worked with their asset protection people to try to gather info. Ended up with the district level people at three of those places. Do you have any idea how much stuff gets stolen every year? They call it shrinkage."

"I've heard it's a lot, but I couldn't tell you exactly how much. Someone told me the workers aren't allowed to stop anyone."

"Right because if anyone gets hurt, then it becomes a much bigger problem."

"One of the district people said that the shrinkage can be anywhere from half a million to a million depending on the store."

"Wait, a million per store?" Dick asked.

"Mind boggling, isn't it?"

"So, getting back to the case. This is a well-organized thing, but still falls in my department because the individual items are low numbers, and we have to work with those corporations. I keep trying to get rid of these things."

"I don't blame you. What did you find out?"

"I had a lead on where they might be storing stuff. Kinda stumbled into that information because a guy stole some stuff from Walmart and then blew a tire a block away. He tried to ditch the van, but an officer saw the blowout and went to help. When the guy took off running, they caught him. The van turned out to be stolen. He held out through the night and then gave up an address down on the north riverfront. It took me a full day to get a search warrant because the judge wasn't confident in my leads, and he said he didn't want to hassle citizens. Another judge signed it the next day. When we got there, the place was empty."

"Nothing at all?"

"Nothing. We could see tracks in the dust that came from a forklift and there had been pallets there not too long before we got there. It was a single-story brick building and the owner turned out to be a real estate investment firm from out of state. They're buying up whole blocks in hopes of redeveloping run down neighborhoods."

"Must be nice to have that kind of money. I'm guessing they hadn't rented it out?"

"No. They said they leave them empty to drive up expenses."

"Alright. Then, I'm guessing nothing else came from that?"

"That all went down about two weeks ago. Nothing new since then."

"Got it. I need to take some time to think on this, Carl."

"That's fine. These old fashioneds are starting to kick in."

"Getting a ride home?"

"I'll have someone from the station swing by and get me."

"Good plan. Can we meet up tomorrow sometime?"

"Sure. Let's do lunch at Applebee's on High Street."

"Applebee's? No thanks."

"I'm not making the big bucks like you."

"I'll pay, but let's go to Great Southern Fried Chicken instead."

"That's good stuff."

"Agreed," Dick said. "Quarter after one?"

"That'll work."

Dick finished his drink and slid out of the booth.

"Taking off?" Laura asked when he got to the bar. "Linh said you've got his tab?"

"Yeah," he said and put two hundreds on the bar. "Will that cover it?"

"One of those will do."

"I don't think he's done. See if you can get him to eat something. You and Linh can split whatever is left."

"Trying to buy us off?" she said, and he saw mischief in her eyes.

"Not sure what I could buy. You already told me you talk."

"Good point. Have a good night, Dick. Tell Jen I said hi."

"Not going to see her tonight, but I'll tell her when I do."

"I know she's a big girl but go easy on her."

"Ok."

"Bye, Dick."

He tipped his hat and went out the door.

6

Dick opened his eyes the next morning a few minutes after five. He was alone in his own apartment on the south side of the city. Jen had tempted him to go back there after he left Harry's, but he stuck to his plan. Spending the night with her would have been fun, but getting seven solid hours of sleep was what he really needed to prepare for the day.

"Up and at 'em," he said, but didn't move. "Well, maybe another thirty minutes won't hurt anything."

He closed his eyes and rolled onto his side. He thought about Jen and then the woman from the co-working space. It didn't take long for him to drift back to sleep.

He woke up to an alarm blaring at eight. It was the repeating buzz kind. He realized it was coming through the wall from the apartment next door. The idea of renting a house instead began to seem like a good idea. Maybe he'd call Jack Nelson.

Thirty minutes later, he locked the front door and went to the elevator. His routine of shit, shave, and shower never failed him. Although, a few of his friends had argued that shave should go after the shower. He was a straight razor guy, so he liked the shower last.

"Looking sharp today, Dick," said one of his neighbors coming down the hallway.

"Oh, hey, Doug," Dick said. He didn't like Doug very much.

"Looks like you got a new suit. Men's Wearhouse?"

"It's probably a year old. Attolini, though. Not Men's Wearhouse."

"Sounds Italian. Must be fancy."

"I guess."

"I'm more of a Kohl's guy. No one can tell the difference anyway."

"You might be right," Dick said, inwardly cursing the elevator for taking so long.

The elevator gave a beep and the doors slid open. Doug stepped in and pushed the button next to the G.

"You are going to the first floor, right?"

"Yes," Dick said, taking the corner opposite him.

Mercifully, Doug's phone rang just as the doors were closing. He stayed on the call until Dick could get away from him in the lobby. Dick made his way outside to the covered section of the parking lot. He paid an extra fifty a month for that privilege, but he figured that was worth a few extra bucks.

He was in his truck before it registered that he still had a few hours until lunch with Carl. His desire for routine was strong, so he hadn't thought about anything else while he was getting ready. Now he needed something to do.

"Breakfast would be a good start," he said to himself. "I wonder if Jen is home."

He picked up his phone and scrolled to her name. He hesitated with his thumb hovering over the screen. Then, he pressed the button on the side to turn off the screen.

"Coffee at the work share place. Maybe she's working."

He made his way through town and ended up taking the same parking spot he had used on his last visit. When he walked in the front door to the building, he unsuccessfully fought a smile. She was indeed working and somehow looked even better than last time.

Her hair was pulled back into a high pony, but it looked luxurious instead of relaxed. He made his way to her desk. She didn't look up from her screen until he was almost to her. Her smile met his.

"Back again?" she asked.

"It does look that way," he said and glanced at her nametag. It was an oval brass plate. Her hair had been covering it the last time. "Jasmine."

"Who are you here to visit today?"

"I wanted to get some coffee and maybe a muffin."

"Your reasoning seems a little thin, but I'll allow it. The coffee isn't worth coming here just for that."

"It's not bad."

"It's not good either."

"Do you need my identification again?"

"It would be hard to forget you," she said. "I mean, it's hard to forget your name."

"Right. I think we're both making weak excuses now."

"Maybe."

He took a business card from his inside jacket pocket and put it on the counter.

"Here's my number. Let's get a drink sometime soon."

"I'm still engaged."

"It's just a drink."

"Dick. It is never 'just a drink'."

"Smart lady."

She picked up the card and slipped it in her pocket.

"Are you getting your coffee to go?"

"No. I'll be here for a little bit. Lunch date is my next stop."

"Another woman you met on your adventures?"

"I wish. An old cop."

"That sounds awful."

"Welcome to my world."

"Well, I get a break in thirty minutes. Maybe, just maybe, I'll come up for a cup."

"I'll be there."

"Ok," she said and typed his name into her sheet. "Now, go away. I can't have people loitering at my desk."

"Wouldn't want that," he said. He flashed her a smile and turned for the stairs.

There were only two people ahead of him in line at the coffee shop.

"I'll take a blueberry scone and a large, black coffee."

"Yes, sir," the young woman at the register said. "Would you like to round up for Toys for Tots?"

"That's fine."

"Eight dollars."

"Keep it," he said, after handing her a ten.

"Thank you," she said.

She made the change, stuffed the two ones in the tip jar, and selected a scone for him. Another worker set the coffee on the counter just as she folded his pastry bag shut.

"Have a great day."

"You, too," he said.

He went to the seating area and scoped it out. Only three tables were unoccupied, so he took the one closest to the coffee shop on the right-hand side. He set his briefcase on the floor next to him before turning his attention to the scone.

A few minutes later the scone was gone. Half of the coffee was, too. His phone gave a single, faint ding. He normally kept it face down to avoid wandering eyes seeing something, so he flipped it over to check the text.

It was from Lauren, one of his friends from some charity work he had done shortly after leaving the military. She worked at one of the local radio stations. Her text was a request for a phone call when he had time.

"Must be serious," Dick said and tapped the phone icon.

He scrolled down, found her name, and hit it.

"Hey," she said.

"What's up?"

"Are you taking new cases right now?"

"I'm always listening. Can't say I'm always taking them."

"I see," she said. "I've got a coworker who is in a bit of a jam. Thought you might be able to help him out."

"What's he got going? Cheating wife? Something interesting, I hope."

"No, his wife is a saint. Part of his record collection was stolen."

"Wait, is this Donald Mueller? He emailed me a couple days ago."

"Oh, he did? Yeah. I gave him your address."

"I told him I'd reach out in a couple days. I'm pretty busy at the moment. Honestly, it sounds like a police matter."

"Yeah, they tried that. They took statements, had a look around, and said they'd do what they could. He's not ok with that."

"High dollar stuff?"

"I mean, he's been collecting for thirty years. He said some of them are valuable and others are just records he loves."

"Alright. I just finished one case. Hoping this one doesn't take too much longer but tell him I really will be in touch early next week to see how things are going. Tell him not to pull his hair out."

"Shouldn't be a problem."

"How's things with you?"

"Eh, same old. Started a new gig here on the morning show a few months ago. Adjustments are tough. Not to mention having to be here at four in the morning versus noon."

"That sounds rough. You like it though?"

"Yeah. It's pretty cool."

"Nice. I'll check it out one of these days," he said. Jasmine appeared at the top of the stairs, looking around the seating area. "Talk to you next week, ok?"

"I'll look forward to it, Dick."

"Bye, Lauren."

"Hey," Jasmine said, walking up to his table. "I've only got fifteen minutes."

"You want a drink?"

"Nah. I've got water at my desk."

"So, you came up just to see me?"

"Don't get too excited, big boy. Mind if I sit?"

"I suppose. Ok, so, tell me about the fiancé."

"That's what you want to lead with?"

"It's what you've brought up both times we've talked."

"It's your fifteen minutes," she said. "He's a nice guy. Good job. We've been together for five years and engaged for the last ten months."

"When's the wedding?"

"Haven't set a date, yet."

"Doesn't sound very serious."

"Serious enough for me."

"But the ring keeps other guys at bay?"

"Most guys."

"Jewelry has never deterred me."

"Obviously," she said. "Anyway, what else can I tell you? Or is it my turn?"

"What's your drink of choice?"

"Jack and Coke."

"Not diet?"

"Absolutely not."

"Noted. I'll get some for my place."

"Getting ahead of yourself, aren't you?"

"Being prepared is important."

"My turn, then. Do you have a girlfriend, a fiancé, or a wife?"

"None of those."

"I call bullshit."

"Am I that good of a catch?"

"Well, either you're lying, or you are a womanizer."

"One extreme or the other, then?"

"Probably."

"I'm not married, so you can draw your own conclusion."

"I will."

"What else do you want to know?"

"How long have you been a private investigator?"

"A long time."

64

"How old are you?"

"Thirty-nine."

"Oof."

"Too old for your taste?"

"Never been with a guy that old."

"Oh, now you're going to be 'with' me?"

"I didn't say that."

"What else?"

"Are you the wine and dine type or just go straight at it?"

"Depends on the situation."

"Lots of experience then?"

"Entrapment isn't a nice thing to do, but I'm not a virgin. Is that what you were getting at?"

"Not exactly, but ok. I've only got a couple more minutes to get back downstairs. I will say you are different from Reggie."

"The fiancé?"

"Yeah. He's reliable."

"Sounds boring."

"No comment. Want to walk me to my desk?"

"I do."

"Good," she said, getting to her feet.

Dick grabbed his briefcase, wadded up the bag from his scone, and picked up his coffee. They started toward the stairs. He dropped his trash in a can at the edge of the seating area. Neither of them said anything until they got to the desk.

"Don't lose that card," Dick said.

"I won't. Do I need to set an appointment with your secretary or something?"

"I don't have one of those either."

"Ok, well, have a good day. No loitering."

"Get the hell out, then?" he said, smirking.

"Sort of. I have to work and you're a distraction."

"Fair enough. You have a good day, too, Jasmine."

She met his eyes, and he shook his head.

"You're trouble," he said. "But I bet you're good at it."

"If you're lucky, you might find out."

"I can work with that," he said. "Bye."

She gave a quick wave. He went out the door. When he got to the truck, he checked the clock on the dash. He realized he still had lots of time before lunch and nothing to do. He took out his phone.

"Hello," Carl said.

"Carl?"

"What?"

"You busy?"

"Yes. What do you want?"

"Let's take a ride."

"It isn't even close to lunch time yet. I've got two meetings before that."

"Can you cancel them?"

"No."

"Skip?"

"Jesus. What is so damn important it can't wait until after lunch?"

"Well, there's this cop I've been hired to help..."

"Fuck," Carl said. "For the record, I don't have time for this shit. Where do you want me to meet you?"

"I'll pick you up."

"Great. I'm still holding you to lunch, though."

"Deal. Be there in ten minutes."

"I can hardly wait."

The call ended. Dick put his phone back in his pocket, feeling pleased with himself. He left the parking lot and made his way to Carl's precinct. He was waiting outside.

"Need a ride?" Dick asked after rolling down the passenger window.

Carl cursed him under his breath and got in.

"So, what are we doing?"

66

"I want you to tell me about the locations where the three cases you mentioned went down. Do you know the addresses?"

"We've been over this. I don't memorize my cases."

"Ok. Do you remember roughly where they are?"

"Sure. What do you want to see?"

"How about the warehouse where the box store items were being kept?"

"Turn left out of here."

Dick did. They had only driven for a few minutes, when Carl pointed to the right.

"Pull in there."

"We can't be there yet."

"No, but I want a coffee."

"As you wish, King Friday," Dick said and turned in.

Eight minutes later, they were back on the road. Since Dick had offered to pay, Carl went with the Mega Caramel Latte. It was a monster of a drink. Dick figured it was about a quart. He kept it simple with a Mini black coffee. The Mini was still sixteen ounces.

They took the interstate for a little while, before exiting into an industrial part of the city. Dick followed Carl's directions until they were a couple blocks away. He pulled over when they could just see the corner of the building.

"So, I don't want to hesitate near the building in case someone is watching. I'll take a pass in front of the building and then come back from the other direction. You tell me if anything looks different."

"You don't want to get out?"

"Not really. If someone is guarding the place, they'll notice a truck going by too slow. Getting out gives them a look at us plus an easy way to take down my plate. I don't want that."

"It's your show."

Dick checked for traffic coming up behind him, but there was nothing. This whole road was quiet, but in need of major repairs. Since it was in part of the original city, he figured it had been housing at some point a long time ago. Now, semis were the regular users, and these streets were just recipients of a new coat of asphalt rather than real improvements.

"There are cameras," Carl said when they finished their second pass.

"New ones?"

"There weren't any before, so yes. They were put up quick though. I could see the wiring running on the outside of the brick. Wouldn't be hard to disable."

"If they are on, they would notice if the feed dropped."

"That's a big if."

"Well, you said the place was cleaned out when you were here last."

"Correct."

"Probably nothing new to see," Dick said. "Show me where the video game shops were."

"All of them?"

"No, the general area."

"I'm going to need a bathroom break at some point."

"Ok."

"There's a nice Mobil station near one of the shops."

They left the warehouse behind. Dick was able to catch Grand Avenue, one of the major four-lane roads that predated the interstates. The traffic was a little heavier on that road as lunchtime approached. They went through a cluster of fast-food restaurants, along the edge of the grounds of a large high school, and then Dick spotted the Mobil station. He pulled in and Carl jumped out.

"All better?" Dick asked when Carl returned.

"Yes. This'll be you, someday. Then, you won't find it so amusing."

"I can't imagine myself drinking coffee by the quart. Probably not your first one of the day."

"A safe bet," Carl said. "Turn right out of here."

Dick followed his directions and soon found himself in a U-shaped shopping center that probably dated back to the seventies. This one was clearly not what it had once been. The main store at the back of the lot, maybe it had once been a K-Mart, had been subdivided into an Aldi and some sort of kids' trampoline park.

A post office and some other small shops were on the left wing. A video game shop called Gamer Haven, a Chinese buffet, and a resale shop were on the right. Dick drove the truck to a spot near Gamer Haven but didn't turn off the engine.

"What do you think we'll find here that you didn't last time?"

"Honestly?"

"Yeah."

"Not a damn thing," Carl said. "In fact, I don't think we'll find anything at any of these places. I think we've been over this, but I'm doing this because Carla has already spent the money. Figured she might as well get something for it."

"Ok, Carl. The free lunch, too?"

"Yes. Still waiting on that."

"We'll go there soon enough. Should be on the way back to the precinct," Dick said and put his hand on the gear shift. "The flea market isn't worth stopping at either, then?"

"Can't imagine why it would be."

"Do you remember the addresses of the two people you talked to about the flea market?"

"Not off hand."

"I tell you what. We'll go get lunch and then you can call me this afternoon with the addresses. Ok?"

"You're the boss. I do remember the flea market was called Dave's Treasure Hunt. You can probably look that up on your own. Dave is the owner. I talked to him a couple times."

"That works for me," Dick said. He backed out of the space. Great Southern Fried Chicken was only ten minutes away.

"You know I'm not mad at you. I'm mad at this situation. I'm better than this."

"I have no doubt."

"For the flea market scheme, I talked to a guy named Josh and a woman named Leona. They didn't seem to be friends outside of pulling the jobs," Carl said. "I'll send you the addresses this afternoon. It can't hurt anything."

"Thank you."

They rode in silence for the next few minutes. Dick took a spot in the back row of the lot behind Great Southern. It was an old brick building that looked to have been a warehouse of some sort many years ago. The smell of fresh fried chicken and at least two decades of used cooking oil filled the air. They were both starving.

7

Dick woke up around a quarter after nine the next morning. There was no blaring alarm to wake him this time. He wasn't in a big rush, either. His left arm slid to the side and found an empty spot in the bed next to him. He thought for a moment and realized he had gone to bed alone for the third night in a row.

He stopped in the half bathroom off his bedroom to pee and splash some water on his face. He groaned at the face looking back at him. He felt bloated. Fried chicken would be off the menu for a while.

Once in the kitchen, he scooped some grounds from the red plastic container into his coffee maker. It wasn't the best coffee, but it was good enough. It also reminded him of his mom. She drank that kind by the pot on a daily basis when he was a kid.

While the coffee dripped through, he took a quick shower. Eschewing the normal suit due to his plans for the day, he went with a pair of regular blue jeans and a black hoodie.

He poured a cup of coffee while the skillet heated up. Three eggs, some peppers he had chopped up a couple days earlier, and some shredded cheese went in. Not as pretty as an omelet, but it would taste the same.

The toast popped up a minute later and he dropped it on the plate next to his scrambled eggs. A quick grind of pepper and a shake of salt was all he needed to finish up the meal. He sat down at the bistro table that occupied one corner of his little kitchen.

He flipped open his laptop and clicked the icon for his Gmail. He scrolled through some ads before seeing the email from Carl. It was a simple message telling him the names and the addresses Dick had requested. There was no greeting or signature.

"Grumpy even over email. How nice."

A Google Maps search of the addresses showed that they weren't too far apart. He thought he'd try the flea market first. Then, he'd go do a drive by of Josh and Leona's homes. Josh lived in an apartment complex, so that might be more challenging. Leona stayed in a row house a few blocks from Josh.

Once he had the plan in his head, he took his plate to the sink. He gave it a quick scrub, rinse, and dry before putting it on the rack. He downed his second cup of coffee and ran it through the same process. Finally, he retrieved a silver thermos from the cabinet over his stove and filled it up.

Between ten and ten thirty, he sat in the parking lot that served Dave's Treasure Hunt. He watched a total of five customers go in and three came out. Having the place to himself would be useful, but not a necessity.

He had managed to finish off about half the coffee while he waited. This left him with a need. Small businesses didn't usually have a restroom available, but he decided to take his chances. An electronic chime dinged two tones when he opened the door. The first was higher than the second.

"Welcome to Dave's," said a man behind the counter. He wore an orange polo shirt with white, horizontal pinstripes. It was at least one size too small. His thinning hair was pulled back into a short ponytail. "I'm Dave."

"You got a bathroom?" Dick asked.

"Only for paying customers," David said, looking over the top of his comic book.

"You got any Pez dispensers?"

"Through the door at the back. That'll get you to the storeroom. The bathroom is in the back right corner. Don't blow it up."

"Just need to take a whiz. Too much coffee."

"Sure," Dave said. His focus went back to the comic. It was a well-read copy of Batman. "Pez are in booths thirteen and twenty-seven for sure. Might be a couple in 19."

"Thanks," Dick said.

He went through a thin door that swung into the storeroom and then back out into the showroom. The storeroom was about twenty by twenty and had shelves from floor to ceiling. There were knickknacks of all sorts and a handful of toys that Dick recalled from childhood, including a set of Teenage Mutant Ninja Turtles.

After relieving himself in a surprisingly clean urinal with a strawberry scented cake, he made his way back out. He paused to check out the Turtles but wanted to stay focused. When he got to the showroom, he saw that the only other customer was a woman with long gray hair. She was paying for her merchandise.

Dick glanced at the booth to his left and found a number stenciled on the board forming the top of the front wall of it. Number twenty-two. He saw they went up from there, so he worked his way to twenty-seven.

He spotted a clear, plastic shelf along the right wall, which was a sheet of pegboard that had been painted lime green. The shelf held twenty or so Pez dispensers. Dick didn't see anything that stood out to him. Then again, he didn't know anything about them.

Along the two wooden shelves at the top of the back wall of booth twenty-seven were little boxes holding Funko Pops. Dick had never heard of those but found them amusing. He started reading the boxes, finding it odd that the characters looked so much alike.

Halfway through the second row, he found Detective James Gordon. He took it from its spot, gave it the once over, and decided this would be his purchase. Five bucks was reasonable, and the figure reminded him of Carl, although he was sure the old man wouldn't appreciate that.

"What did you find?" Dave asked when Dick sat the Funko Pop on the counter. "You didn't actually have to buy something. I just didn't want the lady with two kids thinking she could mess the place up."

"Got it. I'm good with this."

"You collect?"

"Not yet. This reminds me a little of a guy I've done some work with."

"Must be a real looker if he resembled a Funko Pop."

"Well, he looks like this. I'll let you draw your own conclusions."

"Yeah, I'll pass," Dave said and looked at the tag taped to the box. "Five bucks. The government gets their part, so that makes it five forty-three. Cash if you got it. Don't like cards for under ten bucks."

"No problem," Dick said and took out his wallet. He took out six ones and put them on the counter. "Hey, so I got a question for you."

"Oh yeah?"

"Friend of mine goes to a couple flea markets across the river. He said the scuttlebutt there was a couple shops up this way got hit by some thieves."

"That's what your friend said? Well, this friend is right," Dave said, standing up. "A lot of people are doing a lot of talking, but no one is doing anything to help. Hell, I don't know you. You looking for an easy score? Maybe you grabbed something out of the back room?"

"I'm not here to steal anything," Dick said, keeping his hands on the counter.

"That's what a thief would say. Right?" Dave said. His voice escalated with each sentence. "God damn cops asked a bunch of questions. They watched my video. Even showed them exactly what the people took. Fucking load of shit! They never found any of it because the two people they identified wouldn't give up the third guy. Then, from what I heard, some detective fucking blew it with evidence and the whole thing went to shit."

"I'm just here to get a gift."

"I thought you were here to take a piss!"

74

"That, too."

"Bullshit. I'd recognize you if you were that third guy, but I don't trust a stranger asking questions about things they shouldn't know about."

"You don't have to trust me. I was making small talk."

"God damn insurance company is raising my rates, too! Cops blow the case and I'm the one who gets stuck holding the bag. Fucking situation is probably going to cost me six months of profit."

"That sucks," Dick said.

"Sucks. Yeah, that's a fact. What's your name anyway? The cops might need to know that if you pull something."

"My name's Nolan. My parents were big fans of Nolan Ryan."

"Whatever," Dave said. He popped open the drawer to the register, counted out fifty-seven cents, and slapped it on the counter. "There's your change."

"Didn't mean to offend you."

"Everything offends me these days."

"I see," Dick said. "Well, good luck getting a resolution to this. I hope they get the people that robbed you."

"Sure, Nolan. I'd love to see that happen."

"Alright, then, I'm going to head out."

"Have a good one," Dave said. His tone carried so much vitriol that Dick thought he should probably close down for the day.

Dick took his Funko Pop and went straight to his truck. He was sure Dave would try to write down his license plate, even though he was in the back row of the lot. He turned to go against the arrows painted on the lot, which took him away from the flea market.

Once he had put a couple blocks behind him, he pulled into a parking spot along the side of the street to regroup. He tapped the Maps icon on his phone and pulled up the address he had saved for Josh's apartment building. It was the closer of the two suspects that Carl had shared, so he went there first.

When he turned onto the street where Josh lived, he saw a row of old houses on his left. They were small and all had the same design. He assumed they were part of a blue-collar development that had gone up in the forties or fifties. The other side of the street had been demolished at some point to give way to three five-story apartment buildings.

The buildings were a sandy brown color. The window frames and doors were all painted flat black, leaving little personality. A few residents had hung plants outside their windows, but those splashes of color were the only things standing out against the plain brown structures.

Josh's building was the middle one. Dick slowed down as he approached. He noticed a few kids sitting outside, tinkering with their bicycles. An old man in a rocking chair sat on his porch directly across the street. The kids looked up at him. There was far too much attention on the location at that moment.

The last stop, Leona's house, was eight minutes further away. Dick took a short detour to drive through a McDonald's for a large, sweet tea. It was like drinking candy, but he liked to have one every month or two. It was only a quarter gone when he rolled to a stop in front of his destination.

It was a small, symmetrical house. The front door was in the center of the house with a single window on either side. The white blinds were down on the left window, standing in contrast to the old, graying siding. A narrow driveway ran along the side of the house with a carport at the end of it. There was no vehicle underneath it.

He needed to keep moving, although he hadn't noticed any people keeping an eye on the neighborhood. It was just as likely that someone could be watching from their living room window as standing outside making their observations. He found a spot just over a block away in front of a similar small house with a 'For

Sale' sign in the front yard. He thought a strange vehicle wouldn't stand out as much in that setting.

He gave the key fob an extra click and his truck honked as he started back toward Leona's house. Clouds were drifting in from the northwest. Dick hoped he wasn't going to have to deal with cold rain. A street light came on over a bus stop at the end of Leona's block when he passed underneath.

Dick paused at the covered bench to watch the house for a moment. With the sky darkening, he thought a light would come on inside if someone was home. Nothing happened for a few minutes, so he kept going.

He scanned the neighboring houses when he got to the end of the driveway. Luckily, only one light had come on. It was the front window of a house halfway down on the other side of the block. He couldn't see anyone in the window, so he walked up Leona's driveway. Once he got to the back corner of the house, he was out of view of anyone on the street unless they were at the end of the driveway.

He knelt under the carport to look at a black stain on the worn-out asphalt. It was tacky, but the clouds kept the familiar rainbow of colors from appearing. Leona needed to have her vehicle looked at.

With his sweet tea in hand, he ventured into the backyard. That space was deeper than he had thought it would be, but the back area was overgrown with brush. He could barely see the siding on the house behind Leona's.

A set of narrow wooden stairs went along the back of her house from where the carport stood to a single door in the middle of the house. The back of the house was almost an exact match to the front of the house. A motion light came on over the small porch outside the door, so he moved back toward the brush.

He found a spot halfway between the two houses. With his hood up and pulled tight, no one would notice him unless they were looking for him. He was lucky enough to find a stump to sit on, which he appreciated because the increase in humidity before rain had been getting the best of his knees the last few months.

He sipped his tea and waited. The clouds kept coming, but the rain stayed away. His drink was still only half gone when an orange Chevy S-10 pulled in the driveway. Dick couldn't remember the last time he had seen one of those. He held his spot and soon the headlight went off, followed by the engine.

The driver's door gave a squeak as it swung open. The driver, a woman with blonde hair pulled into a ponytail, walked around the front of the truck. She was wearing blue scrubs. The passenger side door didn't squeak when she opened it to retrieve a few bags of groceries.

She took one in her right hand and did her best to hook the other four with her left. Leona pushed the door shut with her foot and started toward the stairs. She sifted through the keys on her ring with her right hand. The motion light came on when her foot hit the first step, but she paid no attention to it.

When she was halfway up, Dick made his move. Leaving his sweet tea behind, he went straight for the porch. The railing was open on the side, so he would be able to grab her leg with no problem. She saw him come out of the brush and attempted to skip a step on her way to the door.

Unfortunately for her, the tip of her left shoe caught on the last step, and she went down. Landing on her knees, she winced in pain. This brief setback was all Dick needed to get to her. She tried to swing at him, but the bag of groceries took away any threat.

"Stop," he said. "I just want to talk."

"Fuck you," she said and dropped the single bag. He noticed pepper spray on her hip just as she went for it. He slapped her hand away and yanked it from its holster.

"I said stop," he said and tossed the spray into the yard.

"I'll fight you, you son of a bitch."

"Damn it, Leona," he said, causing her to pause for a moment. "I know you were involved in the switch out thefts at the flea market."

"I don't know what you're talking about. I'm going to call the police."

"No, you're not. You and your partners got away with it. Why would you bring any attention back to yourself."

"What do you want?"

"I want to know who you work for."

"I don't know what you mean."

"I've got all night, if you want to play games," Dick said. "I know about Josh. I've been by his place, and I can go there when I'm done with you. One of you will tell me what I need to know. When this all goes down, only one of you will get leniency."

"Bullshit. Nothing is going down because nothing happened. We didn't do anything."

"There were three of you. Somehow the third guy avoided being identified. The cops will be waiting for you to mess up again. They'll be ready next time. I'm betting Josh will help me out."

"I'll call him and warn him."

"Not if I take you with me."

"Good luck with that. I told you I'd fight."

"I remember," Dick said. "I'm not worried about that part. I can get you in your truck with no real problem and then I'll drive it to Josh's. You know, you might be onto something. If I have the two of you together, I bet I'll break one of you faster. Is that what you want to do?"

"Fuck you."

"That's rude, Leona. Now, should we go inside and talk? Your ice cream is going to melt."

"Fine," she said. "I need to unlock the door."

"Go for it," he said, moving around the railing to join her on the steps.

She huffed and found the key to the door. The plastic bags rustled as she tried to open the door. Dick thought she was dragging it out a little.

"Hurry up," he said, "or I'll drag you down the stairs and put you in the truck."

"You wouldn't dare," she said, looking back at him. She saw a look in his eye that convinced her he would do just that.

With the door unlocked, she twisted the knob and went in. Dick followed close behind her, not wanting to give her a chance to try anything. He felt for a switch on the wall inside the door. When he found it, he flipped it up and the kitchen was illuminated. Leona had moved to the counter to unload her groceries.

"Go sit at the table," Dick said.

"What about the ice cream?"

"I don't give a shit about your ice cream. Go sit down."

"Now who's rude?" she said but did what he told her to do. "If you try anything, I'll fight."

"Yes, that's what you said. I'm here for information, nothing else."

"That's what a rapist would say."

"Jesus. Shut the fuck up," he said. "Hold still."

He pulled some long zip ties from the front pocket of his hoodie.

"What the fuck are those for," she said and started to get up. Dick put his palm on her forehead and shoved her back down into the chair.

"Stay still," he said. He knelt and zipped each of her legs to the respective chair leg. With no further protest, he zipped her wrists to the back legs on the chair. She stared up at him, attempting to look mad. Dick saw only fear. He sat down across from her. "Now, let's keep this quick and your ice cream will be fine. Tell me about the third guy."

"I don't know anything about him."

"Lying will only make this take longer."

"I'm not lying," she said. "I don't know anything other than we call him Bill."

"Well, that's a start. Bill what?"

"I don't know. I don't even know Josh's last name. I don't think Bill's name is really Bill though."

"Ok. Is he the boss?"

"I don't think so. He never seemed like he was smart enough for that."

"Who gave the orders?"

"Bill got the instructions, and we did them. Whoever hired us got the stuff and we got paid."

"So, Bill is probably the guy."

"I don't know."

"How many places did you hit?"

"The cops have plenty of leads. You should check the records."

"I'm not a cop."

"That's what a rogue cop would say."

"You watch too many crime movies," Dick said and glanced over at the counter.

Leona had left her phone next to the groceries. Dick walked over and picked it up. He swiped the screen and got a keypad.

"What's the password?"

"I'm not telling you my password."

"Come on, Leona."

"You can try to make me tell you. I won't do it."

"Fine," he said and stepped behind her. He flipped the phone upside down and grabbed her right hand.

"Ow!"

Dick ignored her and straightened out her right thumb. He pressed it against the screen. The phone unlocked.

"It isn't that hard to cooperate," he said. "Let's see. I bet you even have his number saved as Bill."

She said nothing, but he scrolled through and found it a few seconds later. He tapped the name. Then, he took out his phone and typed in the number.

"That number won't work. He changes it regularly."

"Doesn't matter."

"It's useless to you."

"Maybe, maybe not. If it's no good, then you won't be able to warn him. That's good for me."

"You said you aren't a cop, right? You have to tell me if you are."

"That's not a real thing, but I'm not a cop. I do know the owner of the flea market you robbed, though. He's pissed off in a major way. I wouldn't want to be in your shoes right now. Especially once he finds out where you and Josh live."

"Wait, what? You're going to tell that guy where I live? He'll kill us."

"I doubt that. Have someone beat you? Maybe. Take you to court and sue you for everything you have? Sure."

"We haven't been charged with anything!"

"That's not how civil court works. He just has to convince them that he deserves your money. Those surveillance videos should do that."

"I'm not going through that for Bill."

"Good plan. What will Bill do if he finds out you ratted on him?"

"Fuck this shit. This was supposed to be an easy way to make some cash. My job sucks and I'm behind on bills."

"Here's what I think you should do," Dick said. "Go about your life. Don't tell Josh anything. Don't tell Bill anything. Just keep doing your day-to-day stuff. I'm sure you got paid for the job already, so keep that. I don't want it."

"I don't believe you."

"You don't have to. It doesn't matter to me. I have Bill's phone number now, so I can move to the next step of my plan," he said and stood up.

He used his shirt to wipe off the phone before putting it back on the counter.

"This is a metal chair. How am I supposed to get free? Just wait to die?"

"That's a little dramatic don't you think? Someone will check on you when you don't show up for work."

"Are you fucking serious?" she said, spitting her words at him.

"If you behave, I'll cut one wrist loose. Can you do that?"

"Just cut me completely loose."

"Hmm, no," he said and turned for the door.

"Wait! Fine. Cut loose my wrist. I'll behave."

Dick glanced to the counter and saw a cheap wooden block with a handful of knives sticking out of it. He picked out a steak knife and walked behind her chair. She sucked in her breath, expecting him to do something to her. Instead, he cut her left wrist loose.

"There," he said.

He put the knife back in the block and gave it a quick wipe with his sleeve.

"Don't call your friends. Ok?"

"Ok," she said.

Dick walked out the door. The motion light came on. Leona stared after him, thinking he would come back in and kill her. He didn't come back. Eventually, she scooted herself to the counter and managed to get the knife.

Five minutes after Dick left, she grabbed her phone and dialed Bill's number. She hesitantly stepped out onto the porch, but he was gone. The phone rang.

"What is it?" asked a man at the other end of the line.

"Some guy just tried to kidnap me. He's coming for you."

83

"What did you tell him?"

"Nothing, but he has your phone number."

"How'd he get that?"

"My phone."

"You told him my name?"

"I mean. It was an accident."

"Fine. Get out of town. When he doesn't find me, he might come back for you."

"I don't have anywhere to go!"

"That's not my problem."

8

The annoying alarm woke Dick up again the next day. He turned his head to the left to confirm he was alone.

"I don't even know how many days it's been. Feels like weeks. Gotta wrap this thing up so I can enjoy some downtime."

He flipped the blankets back and sat up. It hadn't been a particularly late night, but he still felt tired. He had fallen asleep on the couch watching Die Another Day, the James Bond movie with Halle Berry. That was something he normally tried to avoid.

When he was done with his shower and shave, he stared into his closet. Selecting a suit seemed beyond his energy level at that moment, so he went with a pair of jeans and a Soundgarden t-shirt. Staying with the easy route, he passed on making breakfast. A trip through the Dunkin' Donuts drive through would be good enough. A couple long johns sounded good.

"Yo!" Doug said as Dick stepped into the hallway.

Dick put his key in the lock, gave it a twist, and then checked the door before looking up.

"Hey, Doug."

"Going the casual route today? That's new."

"Not really. I don't need a suit every day."

"Man, that's good. I'd hate to have to dress up every day."

"Looks like you're having a casual day today, too," Dick said, looking at Doug's outfit. He was wearing a plain white T-shirt that was stretched out around the neck. Slightly matted Scooby Doo pajama pants and a pair of green Crocs made up the rest of the outfit.

"This? I just rolled out of bed and pulled on my lucky Crocs. I need some coffee and a donut."

"I hear that," Dick said and looked down at his phone. It had buzzed, telling him there was a news update of some sort. He used it as an excuse to end the conversation. He started typing a text to Carl. "Oh, man. Work stuff never ends."

The elevator door dinged and slid open. Dick stepped to the control panel and pushed the button next to the G. He didn't ask Doug where he was going. He stayed focused on his phone all the way to the front door, although he had abandoned his text on the way down.

"Hey, Dick, quick question," Doug said.

"What's up?"

"Can you give me a ride over to Starbucks? It's a little chilly out here to be waiting on a bus. It'd be a lot easier on me if you ran me over there. I like the one on Harrison. It's not the closest one, but the service is the best."

"Ah, man, I'm already late for an appointment or I would. My clients don't like having to wait."

"Clients? Are you a lawyer or something? I thought you did private security. Like a rent-a-cop type of thing."

"You see a lot of rent-a-cops wearing suits like I do?"

"Yeah. Good point. You must be a lawyer, then."

"Not exactly, but I do have to get going," Dick said. "Good luck getting to Starbucks."

"I'll get there. Might go back in for a jacket."

"Be prepared. That's what I always say."

"Isn't that what the Boy Scouts say?"

"Right. That's what they say, too. See you," Dick said and walked toward his truck. He started it up and left the lot before doing anything else in case Doug pursued the ride further.

He was the sixth vehicle in line at Dunkin'. Still thinking about the next steps with Carl, he called him. The handsfree took over.

"Hello," Carl said.

"Good morning to you," Dick said.

"Sure. What do you want?"

"Where are you?"

Carl sighed and said, "I'm on my way to the station. Gotta get some work done before we go on some hunt."

"Look, I didn't bother you at all yesterday. You should be thankful."

"Oh, I am. I was hoping for two days in a row."

"I think I have some information that might help close this case. Then, you can have all the days in a row that you want."

"That sounds even better."

"Good. How soon will you be at the station?"

"Five minutes. Want to call me back then?"

"No. I'll meet you there. Be there in twenty."

"Absolutely not. I'm not getting my real job mixed up in this thing."

"This *thing* is about your real job. I thought you wanted to keep it."

"Can't you just call me with the information, and we can talk through it."

"That's not how I want to handle this."

"And I don't get a vote?"

"A vote? Is this a democracy now?"

"Obviously not," Carl said. "If you're going to the station, I'll see you there. Bye."

Dick's phone gave three quick beeps, and the line went silent. He laughed.

There was a narrow lot in front of the police station with about twenty parking spaces. A large one was behind the building where all the police vehicles were kept. A half dozen other cars were parked in the narrow lot when Dick pulled in. He chose one of the angled spots on the side away from the building.

He checked his phone one more time, seeing no updates. A case with his tablet in it was the only other thing he had with him. He walked around the back of his truck and across the lot, making his way to the sidewalk along the building. He was almost to the door when he looked up. Carl was standing next to a concrete cigarette receptacle with a fresh Marlboro in his right hand.

"Hey," Dick said.

"Figured I might as well get a couple of these out of the way before we start in on whatever you have for me."

"Ok."

"You want one?"

"No thanks. I can wait."

"It won't take long," Carl said and took a couple powerful drags. Dick watched about half of the cigarette sizzle away. Neither of them said anything until he finished it a minute later. "Let's go in."

"Lead the way."

"Do we need privacy for this or is my desk good enough?"

"Can we use an interviewing room?"

"Probably," Carl said and pulled the door open. "Beauty before age."

"Thanks," Dick said, leading the way into the waiting area.

A young officer with a flat top and neatly trimmed goatee sat at the duty desk. He looked up when they walked in. Dick thought he was far too serious for his age.

"Detective Cooper, would you like me to process him for you?"

"I wish," Carl said. "No, he's providing information on a case. Not a suspect."

"Ah, ok. Let me know if I can help."

"Thank you, Officer Blue. Are any of the interrogation rooms open?"

"Let's see," he said, looking at his monitor. "Three and five are open."

"I'll take five."

"Ok. What case should I put down?"

"I'll take care of the paperwork," Carl said.

"Very good."

Carl swiped his card near the panel next to the door leading to the back area. There was a pop. He pulled the door

88

open and gestured for Dick to go in. They walked through a wide-open area that had a grid of desks in it. Four across and eight deep. The odd rows faced the back of the building, so they butted up against the even numbered rows. A single metal chair was at the left end of each desk.

They turned right just after the last row and went down a short hallway with steel doors on either side. Small, wire reinforced windows were the only openings in each door. White numbers were painted at the top of each door. The odd numbers were on one side and the even on the other. Room five was the third of four doors on the right.

Carl swiped his card again and the door unlocked with a short buzz. He gave the knob a twist and pushed it open. He led the way in, taking a seat at the far side of the rectangular metal table. Dick took the opposite side.

Carl glanced up at the security camera and said, "Officer Blue?"

"Yes, sir," Blue said in a quick response.

"Turn off monitoring, both audio and visual for five. I'll call if I need it back on."

"Yes, sir," he said. A moment later the little red light on the camera went off.

"That kid's a character," Dick said.

"He's a good one. Still believes in the handbook completely. I give him three or four years before he really starts learning what this job is about."

"Think he'll burn out?"

"Nah. I think he'll be alright. He just has to settle in. Just came out of the Army a few months ago. Still used to the rules."

"I see."

"You said you were Army, right?" Carl asked.

"I said military."

"Right, but you didn't tell me which branch."

"Correct," Dick said. "It's not relevant to the case."

"Most guys I know wear their branch on their sleeve."

"I'm not most guys, I guess. Now, let's get down to it."

"Sure. Business first."

Dick took out his tablet and typed in the password. He tapped at a couple icons and swiped through his notes to the correct page. He spun it around and slid it across to Carl.

"Do you recall that number for Bill, the third member of the flea market robberies?"

"First, I never had the name Bill. They wouldn't give him up. How'd you get it?"

"Doesn't matter."

"It does to me."

"Carl. You don't want to know everything I do. I promise."

"Something illegal then? Did you kill someone?"

"Kill someone?" Dick said with a laugh. "Nothing quite that extreme. I persuaded someone."

"Are they in the hospital?"

"Look, Carl, you're going to have to trust me on this one. No one is hurt."

"Fine, but I don't have to like it."

"True."

"Well, if I didn't have the name, then I am pretty sure I wouldn't have had the phone number."

"It's from way out of the area, so probably a burner."

"Makes sense. Doesn't seem like a big enough score to actually be from out of town. We'll have to go to my desk if you want me to confirm whether we have this number or not. I can't access the files in here."

"Sure, would be handy to have a laptop."

"Not for me."

"Before we go out there, can you tell me who all has access to your files?"

"Captain Shannon is the only one on the flea market case. Any officer that gathered information had to run it through me. If they want to see something, the Captain or I have to grant permission."

"And you haven't granted any permissions?"

"Not on this one. I try to make a habit of keeping my information locked down."

"That's a fine plan," Dick said. "You don't think Captain Shannon would share any information with a suspect, do you?"

"You're going to piss me off, Dick."

"I have to ask."

"No, you don't. I've known Shannon for two decades. Way before he was my boss. No way he'd do something like that."

"I'll consider that avenue closed."

"Yeah, you will."

"All right. Do you have a way to get Bill's phone records?"

"That'll take a warrant."

"Makes sense. How about finding a way to triangulate the cell number? Can you get the 911 system to do that without a warrant."

"That would fall in the gray area, but we could do it," Carl said, staring at the tablet. "I think I can do one better though."

"I'm all ears."

"I've got a guy that can track where the phone went over a set period of time."

"That doesn't sound sketchy at all," Dick said, leaning back in his chair.

"Well, if I'm not doing the search, then it isn't the same."

"How do you explain knowing the information?"

"I'll tell them that either Josh or Leona gave it up. They'll deny it and it will come down to my word versus theirs."

"And you thought I was operating on the fringes."

"Do you want to do it or not?"

"I think so, but I don't have anything on the line."

"I gotta break something loose. Otherwise, I might as well hang it up."

"Good. The next thing is that you can't put Bill's number in the computer."

"Why not? That goes against protocol."

"With the plan we have in place, I doubt that omitting a phone number is your biggest concern."

"Fine."

"What I want you to do is put a new number in for Bill, only it will be to a Tracfone I bought at Walgreens last night."

"To what end?"

"You want to solve the flea market case, right?"

"Yes."

"I'm trying to solve the case that Carla hired me for."

"Right. The Defective Detective."

"I don't think you are, and I want to prove it."

"But we can solve the flea market in that process. Right?"

"I think so."

"I'm in."

"Do you want to write down the number before we get out there?"

"Yeah," Carl said, and Dick handed him the phone. The information sticker was still on the screen, so he wrote it down in the little notebook he kept in his pocket. "To my desk, then?"

"Yep. Let's see where the magic happens."

"Please don't ever say that again. My dad used to say that about his bedroom when I was a teenager."

"Could be worse."

"Sure," Carl said, "but you can find some other way of expressing yourself."

"Deal."

They both got up and went to the door. Carl swiped his card and the door unlocked. They walked back along the hallway to the room full of desks. There were only three officers in the room and one person handcuffed to a desk. No other detectives were in the back row, which was where Carl's desk was.

Carl pulled out his rolling desk chair, gave it a quarter turn, and plopped down. He sighed and gave the mouse a shake to wake up the system. The screen went from an image of a rotating badge to a login screen that hadn't been updated in a decade. He typed in his badge number in the username field and then hesitated.

"Fuck," Carl said.

"What?"

"We have to change this god damned password so often, that I can never remember it. Some magical combination of capitals, lowercase, numbers, and special symbols. No space though! God forbid that."

"Focus, Carl."

"Right," he said and flipped his keyboard over. There was a small pink Post-it note on the bottom with writing on it. He studied it for a few seconds and then flipped the keyboard back over.

"Are you fucking with me right now, Carl?"

"What?"

"You keep your password on the bottom of your keyboard?"

"It's handy."

"Yeah, for anyone who wants to use it."

"Who is going to use it? It's a police station. Not like someone off the street could just walk in here and start working. Besides, they'd have to know my badge number."

"You're killing me, Smalls."

"Smalls?"

"Never mind. Keep going."

Carl finished logging in and opened the database with his case files. He searched for the flea market case.

"See, when I click here, it shows my recent changes. So, anything done in the last seven days is easy to see. If someone had changed my information, I'd know. Nothing on this case."

"Hmm," Dick said. "What about recent logins? Does it show the last time you were on the system?"

"I think so, but what good is that?"

"Humor me."

"Ok," Carl said and started clicking tabs. After a few minutes, he found a list of login times. "There it is. This is my first login today. I got in a couple times yesterday. How far back do you want to go?"

"Hold on," Dick said. "What's that one from two days ago at one thirty in the afternoon?"

"I don't know. Probably when I got back from lunch or whatever."

"No, Carl, we were at Great Southern until after two. Remember? The free lunch you had to have?"

"Oh, right. Must be an error. This system messes up sometimes."

Dick looked at Carl's desk and slid the keyboard back. His finger came down on a large paper calendar. An entry written in red ink said 'Lunch - 1:15'.

"You basically advertised that you'd be out of the office for a while."

"God damn it."

"Look. I think you've got a bigger problem than you thought. You aren't defective. You've got someone stealing your information."

"But who would do that?"

"We'll figure that out, but we have to be careful," Dick said and scanned the room. The other three officers were still doing paperwork. None seemed to be paying any attention to them. "It might sound crazy, but I think someone is tipping off your suspects and probably getting paid in the process."

"That's a big leap based on a single login."

"I'm sure there are plenty more. You just didn't know to look for them."

"So, it is on me," Carl said, throwing his hands in the air.

"No. It isn't. Sure, you made it easier for them, but you aren't the first person to keep a password in an unsecure spot. In fact, it makes my job a lot easier when people do that."

"I don't want to know any more about that."

"Look, Carl, all they have to do is log in and look at that tab with recent changes. They don't even have to try to throw you off of anyone in your search. They just steal your phone numbers or addresses and then warn the people. That's got to be worth a pretty penny."

Carl scooted his chair back and stood. He stared down at the calendar for a few seconds and then walked to the wall to his right, which was just past the neighboring desk. He looked at some announcements stuck to a bulletin board and then started punching it out of nowhere. A couple pushpins flew out and papers started drifting to the floor. Two of the other officers jumped up, but Carl stopped punching. He looked at his raw knuckles. One of them had a minor cut on it.

"I'm fine," he said, looking at the other officers. "Just a little pissed off."

"I see that," one of them said and they each took their seats.

"Better now?" Dick asked after Carl sat down.

"Not really."

"Ok, well, reel it in for a little bit longer."

"I'll try."

"Good. Put the number for my burner in the system under Bill's name in the case file. Whoever is accessing the files will see it and try to make another score. I'll be on the other end waiting to set them up."

"Let's make up another appointment for my fucking calendar. Then, we'll know to be ready for the call."

"Make it a breakfast meeting for ten, tomorrow morning. Come here first and check everything out to see if anyone has logged in during the night."

"Got it."

"Call your guy and track down that phone number this afternoon. If I had to guess, he's killed it. The person that gave me the information would have been smart not to tell him, but I think they are loyal to a fault."

"It won't matter. Even if the phone is broken in pieces and thrown in the sewer, I can see where it went up to that point."

"I'll call you once I get the call."

"If you get the call."

"It'll happen."

"Ok. I need a drink. Want to go over to Ironclad?" Carl asked.

"It's not even noon."

"So? It's already been a rough day."

"Look, Carl, you gotta keep it together for another day or two. We're going to figure this out. Work a case or whatever this afternoon but go easy on putting info in the system. Tonight, have a drink at home."

"At home? They say people who drink alone have a problem."

"You drink alone in public, so I don't see how it matters for one night."

"Fine. I'll put on a show for today."

"Want to walk me out?" Dick said, getting to his feet.

"Blue will let you out."

"Ok. I'll talk to you tomorrow."

"Yep," Carl said, and Dick started walking away. "Hey."

"Yeah?"

"Thanks."

"Sure thing," Dick said and went to the door. Blue gave him a wave and buzzed him through.

He went to his truck and slid in the driver's seat. Finding a resolution always felt good, but someone crooked in the precinct was more than he had bargained for. He unlocked his phone and scrolled down to Jen's number. He tapped it and waited.

"You've reached Jen," the voicemail said. "I'm probably working or sleeping. Leave me a message."

"Hey, Jen. It's Dick. Hadn't talked to you in a couple days, so I wanted to check in. Give me a call when you get time. Later."

9

Dick woke up the next morning feeling well rested. It had been a few days since he felt like that, and it was nice. He yawned and stretched his arms out to the side. His left hand brought a soft smack when it struck skin.

"Hey! What the fuck?"

"Huh?" Dick said and looked that way.

Olivia was lying on her side, looking at him. She smiled. He offered a satisfied sigh.

"Do you smack everyone you wake up next to?"

"Only the special ones."

"Not sure that's a compliment," she said and tugged the sheet down. Dick's eyes followed.

"No wonder I feel so good this morning."

"You forgot already?"

"I thought it was a dream."

"You're ridiculous," she said. "What time do you have to work?"

"My first stop is at nine. What time is it?"

"7:26."

"Excellent," he said and rolled to his left, pinning her under him. "Care to kick the day off with another round?"

"A girl could get used to this."

He slid up and she gasped.

"Just not too used to it," Dick said.

Twenty minutes later, Olivia was sitting on the bathroom vanity watching Dick shower through the glass doors. She was still naked, and Dick stole a peek every minute or two.

"Why'd you call me?" she asked.

"What?"

"Why'd you call me last night? Just a quick fuck?"

"Don't make it sound so crass. You knew what it was going to be when you agreed to come over."

"One and done, though?"

"Don't go thinking we're going to start dating or something. I can't do that."

"Detectives don't have girlfriends?"

"This one doesn't."

"I see."

"Just being honest with you. If you tell me no the next time I call, I'll understand."

"Can't see that happening, but ok."

"You want some coffee?" he asked.

"Smooth transition."

"I thought the last topic was finished."

"Yeah. I'll take some coffee," she said and hopped down from the vanity. "Mind if I have a quick shower before I go?"

"If you want to get in now, I'll help."

"You are quite the gentleman."

"I do what I can," he said and slid the door open. She joined him.

Coffee, toast, and eggs made for a quick breakfast. Dick walked Olivia to her car, where he took a kiss.

"Call me again sometime?"

"Count on it."

"Good," she said and got in.

He pushed the door shut. She gave a single wave. Once she backed out, he went to his truck and called Carl.

"Where the hell are you?" Carl asked. "I thought you were meeting me at eight."

"Pretty sure it was nine."

"Did you have something else going?"

"You could say that."

"Right. You don't seem like the early morning meeting guy."

"Carl. I know you're pissed off, but you need to take it down a notch. I'm on your side."

"Did you get the address?"

"Not yet."

"I sent it last night," he said and paused. Dick heard some mumbling. "Ok, there. I guess I didn't hit send."

"That does help."

"Fucking phones."

"Definitely the phone's fault," Dick said. "Ok. I have the address. I can be there in fifteen minutes."

"Good. Come around the block to the alley. He's got a workshop set up in his garage."

"See you in a bit," Dick said and hung up.

Carl's friend lived in an older part of the city. Dick had one neighborhood in mind, but it turned out to be a few blocks closer to the river. That left him in an area with houses from the early nineteen hundreds instead of the sixties. They were in varying stages of disrepair. Many of them had 'For Rent' signs in their front yards.

The alley had once been asphalt. Now it had deteriorated to a mixture of blacktop, gravel, and dirt. Decades of runoff from an old garage had washed a channel along it that left Dick bumping along even at the slowest of speeds. Carl was standing outside a narrow building with Insulbrick siding smoking a cigarette.

"About time."

"No wonder all the guys at the precinct like you so much, Coop."

"Fuck you."

"Worth it," Dick said. "Should we go inside?"

"Yeah," Carl said and sucked down the last of his cigarette. He dropped the butt, crushed it with his toe, and blew out a cloud of smoke. "Prepare to be amazed."

"I can hardly wait."

Carl led the way inside. The gray steel door with no window looked new compared to the rest of the building. The garage door was completely hidden from the inside by bulletin boards and a ring of old kitchen cabinets that went around the inside of the entire building. It was a mashup of used countertops. There were at least a dozen computers spread around the space. It looked like something out of a conspiracy theory handbook, but Dick was pretty sure the computers weren't really doing anything.

"Clarence, this is Dick. He's the detective my daughter hired."

"I'm aware. I saw him on the surveillance camera," mumbled the man hunched over his keyboard. He was tapping away at a program running with nothing more than green lettering on a black screen. "Give me a minute. Timing is critical on this project."

"My project?" Carl asked.

There was no response. Dick studied Clarence with a passive interest. His curly hair formed a ball around his head, with a tiny bald spot at the crown. He wore a cheap, blue hooded sweatshirt and a pair of gray sweatpants.

"Good. That puts the wrap on that," Clarence said. He turned to face them. "Now, let's handle your little situation."

Clarence's spotty beard and long eyebrows completed the stereotype for Dick. He managed to keep a straight face.

"So, you need an address for someone?"

"Yes," Carl said. "I've got a phone number. I thought you said one time that you can track someone based on that."

"Perhaps. I don't know your acquaintance here. I prefer not to reveal anything in front of strangers."

"He's safe."

"That's what you say! I have to be cautious. He could be a government agent."

"I'm a government agent," Carl said.

"You are a police detective. That is a far reach from the type of government agent that I'm concerned with. You'll have to tell me what you want and then wait outside."

"Are you paying this guy?" Dick asked. "Seems like he's all talk."

"How dare you?!" Clarence said, getting to his feet. He was still six inches shorter than Dick but had a genuine fierceness in his eyes. "I know exactly what I'm doing here."

"I could have paid someone off to triangulate the phone's location by now."

"Triangulate a location?" Clarence said and laughed. "That is child's play! First of all, it will only give you a general location. Second, it only works if the phone is on!"

"The number went dead sometime last night," Carl said.

"Then, I guess we should have triangulated yesterday."

"Every person who uses a cell phone has apps on their phone that use location tracking. They might try to turn most of it off, but you can't quite get rid of everything. I have access to the database that holds the information about where each phone number goes. Once I put in the phone number, it will give me a map of where the phone went during the timeframe I specify. Exact locations! Not the vagueness of triangulation!"

"Good," Dick said. "Now I don't need to step outside. I know your process. Easy enough. Sounds a little sketchy though. Probably not legal."

"Legality is in the eye of the government. They do it and so do I."

"I'm not sure that's how it works," Dick said.

"Clarence," Carl said, "let's get to it. Here's the phone number."

"I do not appreciate the attitude of your cohort," he said, taking the slip of paper with the phone number on it.

"Me neither."

Clarence glared up at Dick for another moment before turning back to his computer. He scanned his thumb and the screen lit up again. He studied the paper and then started typing. The screen flashed twice and then switched to an aerial something like Google Earth. The globe was slowly spinning as the system processed the data. Finally, the screen dove in as if they were skydiving from outer space at hyper speed. The city came into view and then a yellow line started tracing along some of the roads. It stopped thirty seconds later.

"There you have it."

"What do we have?" Carl asked.

"The number was only active for a few weeks and the yellow line is everywhere it went while it was online. It appears he frequented a liquor store on Hemsworth, the grocery store on Jefferson, and a house on Frederick Lane. I'm guessing he lives on Frederick."

"You don't think he lives at the liquor store?" Dick asked.

"You, sir, are a smartass."

"Obviously."

"Ok, ok," Carl said. "Can you give us the exact address?"

"Of course," Clarence said. "452 Frederick."

"Thank you, Clarence. How much do I owe you?"

"A hundred in cash will be sufficient."

"Ok," Carl said and took out his wallet. He pulled out five twenties and handed them over.

"No comment from the fashion model?"

"It's not my money," Dick said. "I appreciate the fashion model comment, though. Been a while since a man of your caliber praised my looks."

"Carl. Please remove this man from my workshop."

"Let's go Dick," Carl said and went to the door. He opened it and gestured for Dick to go first.

"Have a grand day," Dick said.

"Ha!" Clarence said and turned away from him.

Dick walked to his truck. Carl was two steps behind.

"Now who's being an asshole?" Carl asked.

"That? That was nothing. He had it coming."

"Maybe the people I lose my temper with deserve it, too?"

"Possibly, but not when it's me. I won't put up with that shit."

"So what's the plan? I'd like to go straight to the address he gave us. Who knows how long they'll be there, if they are even still there?"

"They have no reason to be in a hurry. Leona almost certainly tipped them off, but as far as they know I'm just a guy poking around. She didn't give me the address."

"You think they'll be on the move, but not in a rush. I guess that makes sense," Carl said. "I still want to go there this morning."

"Oh, we're going there now," Dick said. "I think we should ride together though. Maybe rolling up in two vehicles would draw attention?"

"Let's take my car. Your beast of a truck stands out in a neighborhood like that."

"I'm not leaving it here. Let me check Google maps."

Dick put in the address Clarence had given them and saw that there was a good gas station where Frederick Street met the main road. That would be safe enough.

"Meet me at Quik Gas n Go. The aerial looks like I can park my truck along the side of the building without drawing attention for a little while."

"I know that place. Good coffee. I'll get a cup while I'm there."

"Thought you were in a hurry."

"Three minutes won't make a difference. Besides, I don't have to pay if I flash my badge."

"That's a good deal."

"I don't complain," Carl said. "Let's go."

They dropped off Dick's truck in a spot between the wooden dumpster enclosure and the side of the building. The air pump was on the other side of the building and a dilapidated Chevy Malibu was in the other space. Dick was confident no one would pay any attention.

"Ready?" Carl asked when he walked out of the gas station with his cup of coffee.

"Waiting on you."

The doors of Carl's cruiser clicked. They got in and Carl took a few long drinks. He checked his phone and then started out along Frederick Street.

"A lot of people home during the workday on this street," Carl said, weaving between the cars parked on either side of the road.

"Maybe they work from home. Maybe they run elaborate theft schemes and don't work in the mornings."

"Such a smartass."

"Looks like it's just around the curve," Dick said, looking at his phone. "Should be a narrow, two-story house on the left. The picture showed yellow siding, but it's three years old."

Carl didn't respond, but he pulled into a spot behind a tan Ford Taurus. He put it in park and picked up his coffee. Dick looked at him.

"Stopping here, I guess?"

"I may be a defective detective, but I'm pretty confident it's going to be the place with a big U-Haul backed in the driveway. We can wait until we see someone outside the house and make a decision. You should have gotten a coffee."

"I'll be ok," Dick said. "We probably won't have to wait long."

Six minutes was all it took.

"You recognize either of those guys?" Dick asked.

"The second guy is Josh, the one I interviewed with Leona. The other guy could be Bill or just another guy he recruited."

"Want to wait and see?"

"Not really, but I don't have a warrant."

"I'm sure you are well aware, but you don't need one if you're outside."

"Obviously. I'm on a short leash, so I don't want to blow this opportunity."

"What would improve it?" Dick asked.

"I don't know."

"Call it in, Carl. I bet your captain will approve."

"Fuck it," Carl said and unlocked his phone. He tapped the station's number.

"Remember. Trust no one."

"Got it,"

"Fifth precinct," said a woman on the other end of the call.

"Hey, Duncan, it's Cooper. Can you put me through to the captain?"

"Hi, Detective. The switchboard says he's on the phone. You want to wait?"

"Yeah. I'll wait. Thanks."

The line clicked and he heard Kenny G take the place of the silence. Carl watched the two men bring out a couple more boxes each. Every box was small with what he would consider to be excessive tape. He thought that was a good sign something valuable was in there. The soprano saxophone music was suddenly blotted out by a strange chirping ring from Dick's side of the car.

"What the fuck is that?"

"The burner," Dick said, reaching into his pocket. "Keep your mouth shut when I answer this. I'm going to put it on speaker, so you can hear everything. If the captain picks up, get out of the car. Ok?"

"Yeah. Yeah. Answer it."

"Hello," Dick said.

"Is this Bill?"

"I think you have the wrong number."

"No, wait," the man's voice said. "I think I can help you out."

"Mother fucker!" Carl yelled and swiped for the phone. Luckily, he hadn't released his seat belt. His fingertips came up a little short of his goal. "Son of a bitch!"

"Shut the fuck up," Dick said.

"What's happening?" the voice asked.

"Get the fuck out. Right now!" Dick said to Carl.

"No way."

"Do it!" Dick said and covered the phone with his hand. "Right now."

"Fuck," Carl said and popped the latch on his seatbelt. He threw the door open and got out. He slammed it behind him.

"Sorry about that," Dick said. "One of the guys that works for me hit his head coming into the room."

"Sounded more like a car door."

"Look, man, I'm busy. Did you want something?"

"Yeah. Ok. I know what kind of business you're in and I've got information for you."

"What does that mean? I'm hanging up."

"No. Hold on. I got your number from a police database. One of the detectives is closing in on you. I can give you more information, but it isn't free."

"Nothing is these days. What do you want?"

"I want a thousand dollars."

"A thousand? A little steep when I don't know what I'm getting."

"It's good stuff. I got your number, didn't I?"

"I guess so. What do you take? Venmo? Never been blackmailed before."

"It's not blackmail. I'm just selling you information."

"Sounds like blackmail, but ok."

"I take cash. Nothing bigger than a twenty. We'll meet in an hour."

"An hour? Pretty demanding. I told you I'm busy."

"An hour or nothing. The cops will be on you before long."

"Fine. An hour. Where?"

"I'll be at the Waffle House on Lightcap Road. You know where that is?"

"I can find it."

"Good. I'll be in a booth along the wall to the left when you come in. I'll be in a Guns 'n Roses shirt. Red cap."

"Got it."

"Put the money in an envelope. I'll trust you not to short me. Otherwise, I'll have to tip off the cops."

"I'll have your money."

"Good. See you then."

The line beeped as the call ended. Dick leaned over and tapped on the driver's side window. Carl bent and looked in. Dick waved for him to get back in.

"Well?"

"Well, what?" Dick asked. "Did you get the captain yet?"

"Not yet. Still on hold. That was Chris Rast. Motherfucker sits four desks away from me."

"Yeah, well, you almost blew it. We're close to finishing this thing. You have to pull it together."

"If you were in my shoes, you'd be pissed, too."

"Yeah, but I'd also know what has to be done to solve this," Dick said. "Just because he's the one calling doesn't mean we have enough to pin it on him."

"Fuck me," Carl said, looking out the window.

"Excuse me?" said a voice from Carl's phone.

"Oh, sorry, Captain."

"What do you need, Detective Cooper?"

"I put together a couple things and I think I have the address of the guy behind the thrift shop thefts."

"You think?"

"There are two men putting boxes in a U-Haul truck. One of them is definitely the guy I interviewed in the initial investigation.

The other one is unknown but could be the unknown third person. We can catch them outside, I think."

"We?"

"Yeah. Dick Wondercock is here with me."

"Why in the actual hell do you have a civilian with you on a case? A private detective at that."

"You know who he is?"

"Cooper. It is my job to know what's going on around this precinct."

"Then, you know he's working for my daughter to figure out why I'm so bad at my job."

"I heard about that. Yes. He still shouldn't be riding along on an investigation. If things go sideways and he gets hurt, they'll nail your ass and mine to the wall."

"His truck is two blocks away."

"Good. He needs to go back to his truck and be long gone before Officers Blue and Vazquez get there. You do nothing until they get there. Got it?"

"So, you're approving?" Carl asked.

"Yes, with the aforementioned restrictions," Shannon said. "I'll dispatch those two in a minute."

"Are you aware that someone is hacking my computer and selling information?"

"Do what?"

"Someone at the precinct is logging into my computer, getting information about my cases, and selling it to the suspects."

"Are you fucking with me right now, Cooper?"

"I'm not."

"Jesus."

"Let me talk to him," Dick said.

"No. You can't talk to Captain Shannon."

"Put him on."

"What?"

"Give him the damn phone, Cooper!"

Carl huffed and then handed the phone to Dick.

"Captain Shannon. This is Dick Wondercock. I was hired to help figure out why Cooper's cases were falling apart. I've been working on this for several days and I think we figured it out," Dick said and went on to explain the details. "The person selling the information called me a few minutes ago. Carl seems to think he recognized the voice of the caller. An officer named Chris Rast."

"Rast?"

"That's what he said."

There was typing at the other end of the call.

"He's off until two."

"Makes sense. He said we had to meet this morning."

"Where?"

"Hold on. I'm going to get out of the car. I don't want Carl to decide to join us. He's a little fired up."

"You aren't taking my phone out of the car!"

"Yes, I am. Stay put," Dick said and got it. He waited a moment to see if Carl would get out, too, but he didn't. "Still there?"

"Yes."

"Rast wants to meet at the Waffle House on Lightcap in just under an hour. He told me to bring a thousand in cash, which I can get."

"No. I'll get you the cash. If this actually goes down, I'll have to take it back as evidence and you probably don't want to lose a thousand bucks."

"I'd prefer not to."

"Ok. There is a McDonald's a quarter mile east of the Waffle House. I'll meet you there to give you the money. You'll have to sign for it, of course."

"Not a problem."

"Then what?"

"I'm supposed to give him the cash in exchange for the information he has on what he believes is my case. He thinks I'm part of the thrift store thefts."

"Right. I hope to God that it isn't Rast. The internal mess this will create is more than I want to deal with. It'll be bad enough if someone simply hacked into the system."

"Had to be someone in the precinct. They used Cooper's computer."

"Shit."

"Yes. I figure I'll go in and make the transaction. Maybe it would be best if you came in a few minutes after me. If it is Rast, then seeing it for yourself might make things easier."

"It would," Shannon said. "It would also make my job easier if you weren't involved in the first place."

"The argument could be made that I am making your job easier by including you at all."

"I guess so. A compromise of sorts."

"I'll meet you at McDonald's in forty-five minutes and then we will go through with the rest of the plan."

"That sounds good," Shannon said. "Not gonna lie. I was hoping for a relaxing day, and this is about as far removed from that as I can think of."

"You might lose an officer, but you're going to gain a detective."

"That's a good way of looking at it, Mr. Wondercock."

"See you in a bit," Dick said and hung up.

Dick parked his truck in front of Waffle House fifty-five minutes later. The lot was only half full, so he hoped Chris would be in the right spot. The Guns n Roses shirt should be easy enough to pick out, if he was sitting somewhere else.

"Sit wherever you can find a spot," said an older woman behind the counter when Dick walked inside.

The front wall of the building was to his left. Each booth was occupied, but the last one had a man in a red cap. Dick couldn't make out the shirt but went to check it out. The man looked up at him when he turned the corner around the end of the counter. Dick nodded and the man leaned back, revealing the Guns n Roses shirt.

"I'm Bill," Dick said.

"Have a seat."

"If you don't mind, I'd prefer to sit on that side. I don't like having my back to the door."

"You've been watching too many gangster movies. Have a seat."

"First, there is no such thing as 'too many gangster movies'. Second, you picked the booth, the location, and the time. You are in complete control. This is my one ask."

"Fine," Chris said. He pushed his cup of coffee and empty plate across the table. He stood, moved around to the other side, and slid onto the bench. Dick took the vacated spot. "You have my money, I assume?"

"I do," Dick said and pulled a thick envelope from his pocket. Chris reached for it, but Dick kept his hand on it. "I want to know what I'm buying first."

"The detective handling your case recently added the phone number I called you on. I think he's getting closer to identifying you. You can definitely throw him off if you get a new number and move to a new location."

"Do I get a follow up call if there is new information?"

"Not if you're smart," Chris said. "I've done this for well over a dozen people being investigated. Everyone follows my advice of getting a new number and moving. Then, the trail goes ice cold. You won't need a follow up call."

"Over a dozen?"

"Yes. I'm not giving you an exact number, but let's just say it has been lucrative for me. Depending on the case, I set a reasonable rate for the information."

"Is that right?" said a man standing a couple steps behind Chris.

Chris turned to see Captain Shannon standing there. The flush in his face increased as the color drained from Chris's cheeks. Dick crossed his arms.

"Do you have a weapon on you?" Shannon asked.

"I do."

"Put it on the table. Don't do anything stupid."

Chris sighed, rubbed his goatee, and took his pistol from inside his jacket. He held it flat in his hand for a moment. Then, he put it on the table without incident. The older woman behind the counter saw it, but Dick got the feeling she had seen a gun in that Waffle House before.

"What now, Captain?"

"This is going to be a mess. If you cooperate, it will be less of a mess. Going to be an internal investigation that will take a while. You're going to prison. Likely for a long time."

"They'll eat me alive in there."

"You knew what you were doing, Chris," Shannon said. He took the gun. "Let's make this easy. You get up, walk out the door, and go to my car. It's in the second spot to the right."

"At least I helped you catch this guy. Right?"

"No."

"Cooper couldn't track him down. This is the guy they called Bill in the thrift shop case!"

"It's not. You got played," Shannon said. "Now, let's go."

"Damn," Chris said, looking at Dick.

"I'm going to need you at the precinct in about an hour, Mr. Wondercock."

"I'll be there."

10

Dick thought it might be a long afternoon, so he stopped at a local burger place for a quick lunch. There were only a few cars in the lot, and they didn't have a drive through. He found a spot and went in.

"Hey, Dick," the waitress said when he walked in. She had curly, black hair with one ringlet hanging down her left cheek. Her navy-blue button down and jeans were a bit oversized, but she wasn't trying to pick up anyone at the restaurant.

"Hi, Sandy," he said and took a booth on the front side of the building.

"Coffee?"

"I'll have iced tea, a bacon double cheeseburger with cheddar, and some onion rings."

"Wow. Loading up today."

"Gotta go in for an interview with the police in a little bit."

"What'd you do now?"

"Nothing they can pin on me," he said and smiled at her. She blushed.

"Frank is working. Your food will be up shortly."

"He makes the best burgers."

"Don't go giving him a big head. I'll be right back with your tea."

"Thanks."

He took his phone out as soon as Sandy walked away. He typed in Carla's name and her number loaded. The phone started ringing as soon as he tapped her name.

"Hello?"

"Carla, this is Dick Wondercock. Are you busy?"

"It's ok. What's going on?"

"Well, it's been a busy few days here. I finally have some good news for you."

"Oh yeah?"

Sandy put the glass of tea in front of Dick with a long spoon and a little tray with a selection of sweeteners. He gave her a thumbs up. She nodded and walked away.

"Turns out your dad isn't defective, as he likes to put it. He was doing everything just fine, but someone was getting into his files and selling information to the people he was pursuing."

"How does that even happen?"

"One greedy cop and one old detective that does a poor job of securing his information."

"Did Dad leave paperwork laying around or something? I thought he said they went completely to computers."

"They did. Let's just say he was keeping his password taped to the bottom of his keyboard. Not too hard to access."

"Jesus."

"Well, I don't think he'll do that again," Dick said. "Do you think you can fly in?"

"Yeah, I think I can do that. Do you need me today or is tomorrow ok?"

"I don't need you at all, other than completing your payment. The guy that was selling the information is someone that your dad worked with almost daily. Not the best of friends, obviously, but he's pretty worked up. I thought maybe a visit for a couple days would be a good way to keep him relaxed a little more than if he was on his own."

"Gotcha. I'm overdue for a visit anyway. Looks like I can get a direct flight tomorrow that gets me in just before noon."

"Sounds good to me. Maybe a call this evening would hold him over."

"I really appreciate all your help, Dick. If there is anything I can do to return the favor, let me know," she said.

"Go ahead and hit send on that payment and we're good," he said. "Maybe we can get a drink sometime, too."

"Works for me," she said. "You'll have the money within the hour."

"Thanks, Carla. Have a good day."

"Bye, Dick."

He tucked the phone back in his pocket and looked out the window. He saw a small SUV with a Salt Life sticker. He thought a quick vacation to the coast might be in order because there was certainly no salt life here.

"Here you go, big boy," Sandy said, sliding the platter in front of him. "I told Frank you said he makes the best burgers, so he rewarded you with a few extra rings."

"That's a good trade-off for me."

"It is if you like onion rings."

"A bacon cheeseburger and onion rings are one of life's perfect meals."

"If you say so," Sandy said. "I'll leave you to it. Try not to get arrested this afternoon."

"The odds are low, but never zero."

"I'll check in on you in a few minutes."

"You should let me buy you a drink sometime."

"Let's talk about that next time. I can't be seen with a convict."

"Fair enough," he said and picked up an onion ring. He took a bite, and it was perfectly crispy. He smiled. Sandy rolled her eyes and went to one of her other tables.

The restaurant got a little busier and Dick didn't get a chance to talk to Sandy again. He left a twenty under his tea glass. She offered a wave from across the room as he went out.

He had to park at the end of the front lot when he got to the precinct. He saw two vans with the names of local news stations on them. A few others looked like they probably belonged to lawyers. He prepared himself for what would likely be a madhouse, especially if Carl had completed his task.

"You must be Dick Wondercock," said the officer at the duty desk when he walked in.

"What makes you think that?"

"This," he said, holding up a picture. "I'll buzz you in."

Another officer was standing just outside the door leading inside from the waiting area. One of the news anchors stood up when Dick approached the door.

"Sit down, Julio," the officer said.

"How does he get to go in, but we don't. We've been waiting forever."

"If you don't want to wait, you can go home."

"Abuse of power, Officer Aubert," Julio said.

"Not even close, but nice try. Come on in, Mr. Wondercock."

Dick went through the door and found the room of desks at almost full capacity. Only four desks were vacant. Most of them had at least two people at them. Carl was pacing at the back of the room. He looked over when he heard the door click shut.

"Where the fuck have you been?" Carl asked when he was halfway to Dick. The conversation around the room calmed to focus on the biggest story of the day.

"I stopped for lunch."

"Seriously? All this is going on and you thought you'd take time to eat?"

"Yes. You need to chill out."

That was when Carl realized everyone was watching him.

"Captain Shannon said for us to go to his office as soon as you got here."

"Lead the way."

Carl went between a few of the desks and then along a short hallway opposite of the interrogation rooms they had used a few days before. The last door had a wired glass in its window and the captain's name stenciled across the middle of it. Carl knocked.

"Yeah," Shannon said from inside.

Carl opened the door and said, "Wondercock is here."

"Good. Come in. Sit down."

117

Dick closed the door behind him. They took the two chairs opposite the captain. Carl sat on the edge of the chair, still agitated. Dick leaned back with his arms on the wooden armrests.

"Today is the worst fucking day I've had in a while," Shannon said. "Having said that, it had to happen. Luckily, Rast isn't challenging anything at this point, but his lawyer has him holed up in one of the interrogation rooms."

"Which one?" Carl asked.

"Doesn't matter, Carl. You're going to stay far away from anything that even smells like Rast."

"I want to talk to him."

"Absolutely not. I'm not letting you have any opportunity to jeopardize this."

"What would I possibly do?"

"God damn it, Carl!" Shannon said and slammed his fist on his desk. "I told you no and that's the end of it. There is going to be one hell of an internal investigation and they are going to be up my ass the whole time. I can see this taking a month or more."

"I just..."

"Shut the fuck up, Carl. Jesus. I know you're pissed, but I don't fucking care right now. This is bigger than you. You need to remember that I didn't lose faith in you, even after you lost faith in yourself."

"I know."

"Then, act like it. You don't get to talk to Rast. Not now, not ever. Even if you get the chance someday, you'd be smart to avoid it. Nothing good for you will come from that interaction. Now, here's what's going to happen. I'm going to take a full statement from you, Mr. Wondercock, regarding everything you did or saw during his investigation. I mean everything from the first time you heard Carl Cooper's name."

"Ok," Dick said. "I had a good lunch, so I'm all set."

"You and your damn food," Carl said.

"Carl, are you done with your report from today?"

118

"Almost."

"Poirot was out there earlier. Did you see him before you came in?"

"I think about everyone is out there." Carl said.

"Good. Find him, get a room, and bring him up to speed on your cases."

"My cases?"

"Yes. The thrift store should be the priority, but I want him to be knowledgeable of all cases currently assigned to you. Make sure he's added with full access to them in the database."

"Why?"

"Because I fucking said so. Ok?"

"Yes, sir."

"Now, I want you to make sure Poirot is set up by the end of the day. Actually, let's say by five o'clock."

"All of my cases and go over the notes by five?"

"Yes."

"I'll try."

"You'll do it because starting at five you are being placed on paid leave."

"I'm what?!"

"I can have you escorted out now, if you want. I'd be ok with that."

"But why am I being punished?"

"It's not a punishment, Carl. Get your head out of your ass for a minute. You're getting paid to take a break. The internal investigators would have done it, if I didn't. So, you should use your time wisely the rest of the day."

"Carla is flying in tomorrow," Dick said.

"What? How do you know that?"

"I have a phone. She has a phone. She hired me. I called her and told her you might need a visit."

"Good call, Mr. Wondercock," Shannon said. "Now, go out there and get to work, Carl. I don't want to hear a peep from you

119

the rest of the day. If one person comes in to tell me you aren't behaving, you'll be escorted out. It won't be pretty. Got it?"

"Yes."

"Good. Get out of here, Carl. I'll be in touch, but don't come to the precinct without my direct permission."

"Ok," Carl said and got to his feet.

"Mr. Wondercock, I need you to stay here with me."

"Call me Dick, but that's fine," Dick said. "I'll see you and Carla in the next few days."

"Gotta get your money. Right?" Carl asked.

Dick ignored that and said. "Oh, I have something for you."

"Not sure how many more surprises I can handle," Carl said.

"Here," Dick said, taking the Funko Pop from his briefcase and handing it to Carl. "Looks just like you."

"No, it doesn't," Carl said, looking at the figure. "Commissioner Gordon? Like the guy from Batman?"

"What do you think, Captain?"

"I can see it."

"You two are both assholes," Carl said. He dropped the toy to his side and went to the door. He opened it, went out, and closed it without further comment.

"Dick, do you mind if I record this? I feel like it could take a while and I'd rather type later."

"Fine with me."

Captain Shannon spent the next two hours with Dick, going over all his notes and experiences from the case. He was surprised by the details offered, although he didn't approve of all the tactics Dick had used. In the end, they would bury the unsavory tactics and Shannon would make sure Carl's password wasn't taped to his keyboard going forward. Shannon even suggested that he could use a detective like Dick on the force. Dick politely declined.

By a quarter after four, Dick was home. It had been an exhausting day. He decided to get comfortable and have a frozen pizza for dinner. He figured on watching a couple movies unless he could get ahold of Jen. He called her again.

"Hi, Dick," she said.

"Hey, there. How are you?"

"I'm ok. You?"

"Finally wrapped up my case. Haven't talked to you in several days, so I thought maybe we could hang out."

"Tonight?"

"Sure, unless you're busy."

"I mean, not technically busy," she said with a sigh. "I ran into one of my old boyfriends the day after we last talked. We had drinks and I've seen him every day since then. I'm not going to lie that it is nice having someone I can see every day."

"I get it."

"I don't know, Dick. You're a cool guy and damn good looking, but I think I need a little more. I don't see how this can work out between us."

"Jen, don't stress over me. I told you this is the way my life works. I'm pretty sure I told you that there would be days at a time, and I wasn't really looking for a relationship."

"Yeah, you did. I just thought maybe it would work."

"I guess I've been doing this long enough to know it wouldn't. I hope things work out with your guy."

"He's not my guy."

"Jen, you're a super cool lady. If you want him to be your guy again, he will be. Do what makes you happy, ok? No hard feelings here."

"Yeah, I guess that's the best I can do. Maybe I'll see you at the bar sometime?"

"You never know where I might show up, Jen."

"Ok. Bye, Dick."

"Bye," he said and hung up.

He went to take a shower before putting on sweatpants and a t-shirt. Lunch was still sitting heavy in his stomach when he was cleaned up, so he chose Tombstone as his first movie of the evening.

About the time that Doc said "Why, Ed Bailey, are we cross?", there was a knock at the door. Dick hit pause and walked to the door. He looked out the peep hole and couldn't believe his eyes. He opened the door.

"Hi, Jasmine."

"Hey there."

"What are you doing here?"

"Can I come in?"

"Sure," he said and stepped out of the way. She walked a few feet past him. He closed the door before turning to face her. "What can I do for you?"

"Ok, so I need some fun in my life. You seem like fun."

"What about Reggie? Is your fiancé not the fun in your life?"

"Shut up. You know he's not. Let's just not talk about him at all. Ok?"

"How did you find my apartment?"

"Have you heard of the internet? Lots of people have access to it. You gave me your business card, so it took me a solid five minutes to find this place."

"And yet it took you days to get here."

"Look. Having the information and acting on it are two different things."

"Do you want a drink? I did pick up your Jack and Coke the other day."

"Maybe in a little bit," she said. "Right now, I want to fuck. Can you handle that?"

"Straight to the point. I like it. I've wanted that since I saw you the first time."

"Yeah, I know you did. I'll assume the bedroom is this way," she said and started along the hallway.

She dropped her coat, pulled off her hoodie, and stepped out of her jeans before she made it to the door. Dick stared at the show, thoroughly enjoying himself. She looked even better than he had imagined.

"You coming?" she asked and unfastened her bra.

"Yes, ma'am," he said, moving quickly to join her. His sweatpants and T-shirt joined her clothes on the floor. She was lying on her side, completely naked, when he rounded the corner. "Wow."

"Yeah, yeah. Get over here."

Dick slid onto the bed and started kissing her legs, then her hips. He continued across her toned stomach and couldn't resist focusing on her chest for a minute before she stopped him.

"Enough of that," she said, rolling him onto his back. "I told you I'm here to fuck. We can play around later, but right now I want one thing. Looks like it's ready."

She pushed him completely flat on his back and then straddled him. You'll get a chance to do what you want in a little while, but right now I'm in charge and you're going to have to be ok with that. He didn't argue, putting his hands on her hips. She leaned forward. Her lips were inches from his. She watched his eyes as she reached down and put him in. His eyes rolled back, and she smiled.